TAKEN BY STORM

by
LINDA KAY SILVA

PARADIGM
Publishing
Company
San Diego, California

Cover Design Copyright © 1991 by Lue Sinclair
Book Design and Typesetting by Paradigm Publishing
Editing by Brenda Hines

Printed in the United States by McNaughton and Gunn

Library of Congress Catalog Card Number: 90-64051
ISBN 0-9628595-1-6

DEDICATION

This book is dedicated to Chlóe, without whom my words and my life would still be chunks of coal.

SPECIAL THANKS

The fulfilling of a lifelong dream does not happen without people who attempt to understand and support our eccentricities. I would like to thank the following people for their unending love and acceptance of the writer in me.

To Rhonda — for uttering those immortal words, "Submit something," and for being the wind beneath my wings.

To P.J. and Tracy — for opening your hearts and your home to me.

To Julie — for loving me in spite of myself.

To my English teachers — for finding the spark and igniting it.

To my Mom and Dad — for giving me the strength and courage to be who I am and to fight for what I believe in.

To the Mother and the Boyfriend — for always warming my lap and my life.

A very special thanks to Deanna and Brenda for caring enough about women's literature to take a chance.

1

As the crisp November air slid through the slightly open window, Delta shivered and rolled the window all the way up. It was a colder California winter than any she'd ever experienced. Usually, she could get by in the winter with wearing only her long sleeved uniform, but not so this year. Watching Miles crank the heater up, Delta smiled.

Reaching over to the radio blabbering numbers and codes, Delta turned down the volume. They hadn't been called to a scene in over two hours, and the most interesting call of the night was assisting a paramedic change a flat tire on the ambulance. The cold seemed to deter even the criminal element, and, for once, Delta was grateful for the quiet.

Glancing over at Miles, her partner of three years, Delta sighed. He needed a slow night as well. She didn't know if he was moonlighting, sharing a second honeymoon with Jennifer, or what, but he'd been awfully tired the last few nights. Whatever it was, Miles did not seem his usual cheerful self. He was coming to work irritable and crabby, often snapping at her for the tiniest of mistakes. Once or twice, she'd caught him napping when she drove. None of this was characteristic of the man who secretly wished he could be Batman, the caped crusader, when he grew up. His recent lethargy and anxiety was beginning to worry her.

Looking over at a sleeping Miles, head back against the head rest, mouth opened a bit, his trimmed, brown moustache twitched in the semi-darkness of the car, Delta smiled to herself. It had taken him nearly a year to grow it. She remembered the day she'd bought him his first moustache comb. When he unwrapped it, he laughed that deep, throaty laugh that attracted so many women. His hearty laugh was a perfect match for his chiseled good looks and static blue eyes. Miles was the archetypal man in blue; a big barreled chest tapering to a flat stomach and taut waist. He was one of the few cops in their station who wasn't overweight or undertall. He looked, to her, strangely like the prototype for the Ken doll and attracted more Barbie look-alikes than any other cop on the road. To Delta, that was most definitely one of the bonuses of having such a charmer for a partner.

Returning her gaze to the empty street ahead, Delta's smile was replaced by a slow spreading frown. There was no question that Miles was one of the few men Delta loved in her life. It was Miles who offered his broad shoulders when she and Sandy broke up. When Delta's father died, Miles and his buddies helped her mother move to a smaller home and safer neighborhood. Not only was he one of her best friends, he was also the best cop she'd ever worked with. In their three years together, they had pulled each other out of tight spots on too many occasions to count. They had always been there for each other. What bothered her most was, where was he now?

Pulling down a narrow alley which commonly slept anywhere from six to a dozen homeless, Delta peered through the darkness and shined her side lamp upon the restless weary crawling away from the light like skittering rats. This meant they were at least alive; at best, it was an indication that none of them had been rolled in the past two hours. They could sleep the remainder of the night in their miserable existence. Delta shook her head sadly.

Turning her lamp off, Delta sighed. If only there was something more she could do to insure their relative safety.

When she first became a cop, her intention was to take her college degree in Social Science and earn enough money to go to law school. But once she hit the streets, she fell in love with the job. Immediately, she enjoyed interacting with the diverse individuals on her beat and loved the energy and vivaciousness of the city at night. Her rapport with merchants and teens alike grew immensely during her first year, so that her beat soon felt like home. Delta also found it incredibly satisfying to collar a criminal after doing her homework on his patterns, motives, and techniques. She never knew life could be so exciting until she became a cop. After less than six weeks on the force, Delta gave up any ideas of law school. It was a decision she never regretted.

Glancing over at Miles, Delta swerved the car so that it rode on the center reflectors.

"How long have I been asleep?" Miles rubbed his eyes like a boy rising from a nap.

"Too long."

Miles groaned. "Now don't start on me again. I'm just not sleeping very well, that's all."

Delta shot a suspicious glance at him. "Oh? And why is that?"

"Damn it Del, sometimes you're a worse nag than Jennifer. I've just had a lot on my mind lately, and I'm having trouble falling asleep. Period. End of subject."

In one swift motion, Delta turned into a parking lot, turned the radio down, unhooked her seatbelt, and turned to face Miles before he could utter a single protest.

"That's not the end of subject. Look, my safety depends on having a partner who is clearheaded enough to make the right decisions. For the past two weeks, you've been walking around in a fog. If you're going to jeopardize your life as well as mine, I at least deserve to know why!"

Bowing his head, Miles stared down at his hands folded neatly in his lap.

Reaching for one of his hands, Delta lightly squeezed it. Playing the tough guy with him had never been easy. Like so many men she knew, Miles was more boy than man. "Miles, we've always been honest with each other. Always. Whatever it is, you know you can talk to me about it." Delta's eyes searched his profile, looking for some clue that would let her into the far recesses of his preoccupied mind.

Slowly, Miles raised his face and forced a grin. "It's nothing, Del, really. I'm bored. I want Vice. I need more action, and I belong there. I want to do more than ride around all night only to arrive ninety percent of the time after the fact. I want to bust real crimes and real criminals. I get so damned frustrated sometimes."

"And you think Vice'll be that much different?"

Miles nodded. "Those guys, they live on the edge. They make things happen. They act, we react. They do, we wait. That's the difference. I want to experience that difference, Del."

Delta released his hand and ran her fingertips over the barrel of the shotgun resting securely next to the radio. They'd had this conversation before; only the last time they'd had it, she and Miles had busted a crack house for a hundred and sixty pounds of the shit. It had made his month. It also showed him how much he wanted on Vice.

"Maybe you need a new partner."

"No way, Del. We're both being wasted on patrol, and you know it. I want us both to go on to bigger and better things, and if I go, I'm taking you with me."

This made Delta laugh. "I'm afraid it doesn't work that way, partner." True to his nature, Miles was steadfast in his loyalty — both on and off the job. Early in their partnership, when they were bringing a suspect to the jail, the admitting deputy pulled Miles aside and asked if he'd been able to "bone the dyke." Miles reached through the opening, grabbed the deputy around the collar, and yanked his face into the glass partition. That was the last time Delta heard any comment about her sexual identity. It was also the first time she knew how deeply Miles cared for her.

"We'll get there soon enough Miles."

"Bullshit. You don't get to Vice by doing time. You get there by breaking open a case larger than life. You get there by putting your ass on the line."

Delta's eyes narrowed. "Is that what you're doing? Putting your ass on some line?"

Miles shook his head. "You know me better than that. I'd tell you if I had something I was ready to nail down."

"Well, you're starting to make me nervous."

Miles leaned back and sighed. "I'm sorry. I know I haven't exactly been a joy to be around."

"It's nothing to do with you and Jen, I hope."

"Nah, nothing like that."

Delta heaved a sigh that equalled Miles's. "Good. I was afraid . . . you know . . . because you were so tired . . ."

Miles reached over and laid a hand on Delta's shoulder. "Not a chance. Besides, the rule is only one divorce per partner per year, remember?"

Delta did not reply.

"How are you doing?" Miles pointed to Delta's heart.

"Okay, I guess. I'm starting to feel a little lonely. Nights are forever when you sleep alone."

"Has Sandy tried calling?"

Delta looked out the window at a couple of women crossing the street. Even hearing Sandy's name stung her heart. "She wanted to go to dinner to talk about buying me out of the house."

"Did you tell her to go to hell?"

"No. I said that I didn't want to see her yet. God, Miles, the most frustrating thing is that she's gone on merrily with her life and I'm still picking up the pieces."

Gently turning Delta so she was facing him, Miles smiled warmly into her face. "Your problem is that you're trying to do it all on your own. When's the last time you've gone out? I mean really gone out?"

"You mean, on a date?"

Miles nodded.

"That last blind disaster."

Both of them chuckled at the horror story behind her less-than-memorable blind date.

"That was almost two months ago. Don't you think it's time you spread out a bit? You're a good-looking woman. How do you expect to get any interest when you stay cloistered away at home or stuck here in a patrol unit?"

Delta painfully remembered returning home because of a stomach flu, and finding her lover in bed with her best friend. Work suddenly became the only real stability in her life; work and Miles. Instantly, all of her friends became suspect as she discovered who had known about the affair, who took Sandy's side, and who had, in fact, help cover it up. One-by-one, Delta crossed names off her social calendar until only a small handful remained; of those, three were cops. That left her little by way of a social group outside of her department.

"I'll make you a deal. I'll start sleeping nights, if you join the land of the living once more and go out. Deal?"

Looking deeply into Miles's twinkling eyes, Delta smiled. He was as close to her as any man could ever be.

"It's a deal. Now can we go catch us some crooks?"

Miles turned the radio up. "Let's do it."

2

Music pounding mercilessly at her temples, Delta glanced at the beer bottle clock on the wall for the tenth time in as many minutes. With smoke clinging to her hair and clothes, stinging her eyes and drifting up her nose, it wasn't hard for her to remember why she didn't visit bars very often. Delta did love to dance and enjoyed being around so many different and beautiful women, but the stale smell of smoke combined with music meant to bust eardrums made her think twice about going out.

"Long time no see, gorgeous."

Cocking her head and looking over her shoulder at the stool behind her, Delta's mouth came to a grin. "Hey there." Eyes scanning the lengthy blonde from head-to-toe, Delta's smile widened. Maybe she could find something worth suffering through the smoky haze.

"I heard about you and Sandy. I'm sorry."

Turning to fully face the blonde, Delta averted her eyes from the long cleavage beckoning her. It had been so long.

"I guess it wasn't meant to be," Delta offered as nonchalantly as she could. She hated these awkward moments of condolence. They made her feel puny.

"Maybe not, but with your best friend? That's harsh." The blonde flipped her hair over her shoulder and scooted closer to Delta. "Are you . . . seeing anyone now?"

Delta sipped her diet soda and smiled over the bubbles jumping out of her glass. The green eyes flirted dangerously with her, and Delta felt a tiny spark anxiously trying to light up.

God, it had been so long.

"Not at the moment."

The woman reached over and gently touched Delta's knee. "Well, if you ever don't feel like being alone, you have my number."

Delta gulped down her soda as the woman swiveled off the stool and sauntered back to the crowded table from whence she came. Glancing slowly around the bar, Delta knew that this wasn't where she wanted to be.

Moving over to the doorway, Delta exchanged pleasantries with a bouncer she had known in college before zipping up her jacket and starting out the door. Almost before her foot hit the pavement, she withdrew it and backed quickly into the darkened doorway.

"Whatsamatter?" the bouncer queried, moving her large frame off the stool.

Delta held out her hand to stop her. "It's nothing. Just a guy I think I know." Peering out from the cover of the darkness, Delta spied Miles across the street, surreptitiously leaving a hooker hotel called the Red Carpet Inn.

"What in the hell?" Delta muttered under her breath. Miles seldom came to this part of the city. What was he doing creeping around a dive like the Red Carpet?

"Anything I can do?" the bouncer asked, leaning against the stool.

Delta shook her head and started out the door. "No thanks." Stepping off the curb, Delta avoided a cab before jogging across the street. Her mind burned with questions. What was going on? The hotel was a rat-infested, bum-inhabited dive. The windows were cracked, the shades were yellowed from smoke and age, and the place hadn't been repainted in years. How it remained uncondemned, she did not know.

She also did not know why her partner was leaving such an establishment at one o'clock in the morning.

Sliding to the corner, Delta peered around it just in time to see Miles cutting across another alley. Instinctively, she reached down and caressed the 9 millimeter strapped to her calf.

Stepping around the corner, Delta came to an abrupt halt. "What am I doing?" Leaning against the old brick wall, Delta released a guilt-ridden sigh. What in the world did she think she was doing? Chasing after her partner on his off hours was the lowest possible act of mistrust. Whatever he was doing, it was his business. Besides, she told herself, maybe it was just a guy who looked like Miles. Maybe Miles had a moonlighting job at the hotel. Maybe . . .

Sighing again, Delta turned toward the parking lot of the bar. Whatever Miles was up to, it was on his time and thus, none of her business.

At least, she figured, not yet.

3

Opening her locker, Delta stared at the two green eyes looking back at her from the mirror hanging crookedly on the inside of her locker door. She had bar eyes; the kind that said a case of Visine wouldn't help. The bloodshot veins were roadmaps weaving around and behind her deep emerald eyes. Delta thought of the many people she'd busted who had eyes just like these. Tilting her head back, Delta released a stream of drops from the bottle. They felt like acid as they splashed into her eyes and then ran down the side of her face.

"One of those nights, eh?"

Looking out the corner of her eye and immediately regretting doing so, because of the intense stinging, Delta nodded to the short Mexican woman standing next to her. Delta's five-nine frame towered over the diminutive Latino known formally as Consuella Dolores Maria Rivera; or, as everyone knew her, Connie.

"Tried to work on my social life last night," Delta said, closing her eyes and returning her head to the tilted position.

"Good for you. Any luck?"

"Nope." Sitting on the locker room bench, Delta opened her eyes and blinked a few times to rid them of the fuzziness surrounding them. "I don't think I'm into it yet."

Connie sat next to her on the bench and smiled. Even in the dull light of the room, her perfect rows of white teeth gleamed. Connie was one of the many Latinos employed by the River Valley Police Department, but her credentials were just as important as her origin. Connie spoke five languages, had a black belt in karate, and was a computer genius. The department considered her a pearl in an oasis of empty shells. Not wanting to "waste" her considerable skills in the streets, they made up a position for her that was suitably titled "Research and Data Input Specialist," whereby, she played on the computer and acted as translator until there was a specific need for her services. This need covered anything from background investigations to developing specific problem-solving software for the department. She had one of the most incredible minds Delta had ever encountered. She was also one of Delta's best friends.

"I don't think there's any need to rush it, do you?"

Delta looked hard into the dark brown eyes smiling back at her. Connie's eyes could dance even when she wasn't laughing or spewing her horrible puns. Although almost forty, Connie could easily pass for her early twenties. Her carmel-colored complexion was smooth and even, and her shoulder-length jet black locks tumbled casually onto her shoulders. She was not altogether beautiful, but there was a girlish charm about her that drew many a woman to her.

"God, Con, on one hand, I'm starting to feel really lonely, and on the other, I just don't know if I have the energy to invest in those getting-to-know-you games. Does that sound stupid, or what?"

Connie reached into Delta's locker, pulled out a bulletproof vest, and handed it to her. "Not at all. It's a good idea for you to take some time for yourself. And when the time is right, you'll know it inside. Lord knows, we never find love when we're looking for it. It has to sort of sneak up behind you and catch you by surprise. That's the Greek tradition."

Delta grinned, pretending she understood the allusion.

"Look at me and Gina. I was alone for nearly five years before I met her."

Delta groaned. She didn't want to wait that long to find someone who wanted to share peanut butter and waffles while playing *JEOPARDY* on television. The house seemed so lonely at times, that she preferred to work overtime instead of going home to the kittens. Even that was beginning to get old.

"And you two met at a car wash." Delta threaded her arms through the vest and pulled firmly on the velcro latches before pressing them down. It felt like a fourteen-pound girdle.

"Exactly. Can't say either of us were looking for a lover. I mean, come on. A car wash? Hardly a place I would consider romantic."

Delta and Connie laughed, sharing the memory of the incident when Connie had to help Gina pull up the top of her convertible just before the car wash started. It was a story Delta had heard her tell a dozen times.

"Love comes to us from mysterious angles, my friend."

"Well, I hadn't actually entertained the thought of going out, but Miles has been giving me a hard time about spending so much time alone."

"Screw Miles! He's been giving everybody shit lately."

This comment prompted Delta to stop dressing and turn back to Connie. "What makes you say that?"

"Lord, Delta, he's been a pain in the ass around here all week. You should have seen him last night. After you left, he was fussing and fighting with one of these computers until I thought he was going to bust it."

"What was he doing?"

Connie shrugged. "I don't know. He didn't seem to want to talk about it. I do know that when Taggart approached him, Miles jumped up and told him to mind his own damn business. It was weird. What's eating him?"

Lacing up her shiny, black shoes, Delta turned the question over in her mind. It took a lot to make Miles angry and even more to make him act aggressively toward someone. Whatever was going on in him was clearly beginning to eat away at him.

"He's just tired, that's all. I don't think he's sleeping well."

Connie shook her head. "No. There's more to it than that. Last night wasn't the first time he was on the computer after work. He's after something, isn't he?"

"I wish I knew. If you hear anything, let me know, will you?"

"In a flash. Well, hon, I've chatted long enough. I haven't put Eddie to bed yet, and I'd better before the Captain sees the great game I'm making."

"Eddie" was Connie's pet name for her computer. As long as Delta had known her, Connie had given her computers names and often referred to them as if they were human. At first, Delta thought she was a bit eccentric, but once they became friends, she realized it was just her nature.

Connie had come from a family of five children in the southern region of San Diego. Once her older brothers realized she had a knack for remembering numbers and calculating figures, they would take her to town and earn the family money by betting people. When Connie was almost sixteen, someone had written to M.I.T. about her mathematical prowess, and she found a scholarship offer waiting for her when she graduated from high school. When she returned home from college, she found that her oldest brother had been killed during a gang war of which he was a member of neither side. It was then that she decided to put her considerable talents to use in law.

"Yeah, you'd better put that silly machine to sleep. Captain catches you and he might pull your plug."

"Oh, he'd like that now, wouldn't he?"

Watching Connie breeze out the door, Delta shook her head. She had been the first real friend Delta found on the force until she was partnered with Miles. And what a partnership that turned out to be.

Together, she and Miles had a nose for in-progress crimes. More times than she could remember, they had stopped a crime as it was happening and made major collars. Those were the most satisfying busts; but Miles was right — ninety percent of the time, they arrived after the crime took place. It was for the ten percent that he lived.

Delta was different. She wanted to be the one called to a woman's house after a rape. If she couldn't have stopped it from happening, at least she could be there to lend some feminine support. If she couldn't stop someone from robbing the little old woman down the road, at least she could hold her hand and tell her that they would do everything they could to get her stuff back. It was the human element that she most loved. And, if they could possibly stop a crime-in-progress, then that was a bonus.

Finally buckling up her belt, Delta looked at herself in the full-length mirror hanging across the room. She had lost weight since the break-up, and her large frame appeared gaunt until she put her vest on.

Adjusting the last of her gear, Delta sighed. With nearly twenty pounds of gear on, she felt more comfortable than when she was wearing her street clothes, which now hung loosely off her.

"I've got to start eating more," she grumbled, staring at the new notch she was using on her belt. "I hope Sandy finds the ten pounds I lost."

Checking her weapon and her ammo one last time, as she always did, Delta started out the door.

"'Bout time Stevens. Captain is chewing the burnin' end of the cigar waiting for you."

"What does he want?"

"Dunno. But you'd better get your butt in there. He's asked for you twice."

Delta inhaled loudly, anticipating trouble. Captain Williams was not one to call her in and ask how her life was. He was more like a principal who called kids in only when they were in trouble. Rifling through her short term memory, Delta searched for any mistakes she might have made during the week.

Slowly entering the Captain's office, Delta closed the door softly behind her. The room, as always, was nearly dark, except for the tiny beam of light shining down from his desk lamp. The room always reminded Delta of a cave.

"You wanted to see me, Captain?"

The large, broad-shouldered man looked up from his report and stared at her. A slow grin crept across his face. "Have a seat, Stevens." Laying his report aside, Captain Williams ran his meaty hands through his thick salt and pepper hair before locking his fingers behind his head and leaning back in the chair. Delta read this posture as harmless and not offensive. Delta believed that posture was the ultimate in truthful communication, and when this particular man was aggravated with someone, he would fold his hands in front of him and rest his chin atop his massive knuckles.

"You've been turning in some excellent reports, Stevens, and that collar you and Brookman made two weeks ago was a fine catch."

Delta nodded, waiting for the other shoe to drop. "Thank you, sir."

"You and Brookman have been working very well together for quite some time now, haven't you?"

"We manage, sir. Some days it works, some days it doesn't." Delta knew what happened to partnerships that became too complacent and comfortable. It was erroneously believed that partners who got along too well weren't on their toes as much as those who argued now and then.

"Except for a few glitches here and there, you're managing nicely." Lowering his hands, the Captain leaned forward against the desk; his hands were folded but rested against his broad chest. "Stevens, I'm all for partners sticking together and showing loyalty, but there are times when it can be extremely detrimental to one partner's health. Are you following me?"

"Yes, sir."

"I've been listening to the hubbub around the station, and I've watched Brookman very carefully lately, and he appears to me to be missing a step."

"Missing a step, sir?"

"Yes. You know, he's been edgy and looks exhausted. What I'm needing to know is, is your partner moonlighting?"

"Not that I know, sir." Delta leaned forward, very aware that her body language was telling him that she would not be cowed into snitching on her own partner.

"I ask you this because some of the men were questioning whether or not he's up to par. Know what I mean? My concern is for your safety, as well as the others' in this station."

Delta licked her lips and chose her words carefully. "If you have a question, sir, why not ask Miles? I'm sure he'd tell you what you wish to know."

Captain William's eyes narrowed. "I have. He tells me he's having trouble at home, but then, I'm sure that isn't news to you."

"No, sir, it isn't." Delta lied. "He's just having a bad week, that's all." Delta felt the sweat form on her palms, as it always did when she was nervous.

"Then you have no concerns that he might be burning out on patrol?"

"No, sir, I don't."

Williams leaned back once more and rested his hairy paws on the arms of the wooden chair. "While I value your opinion, Stevens, I think it's always best to play it safe. I am going to have to consider putting him behind a desk for a few weeks until he straightens out whatever is going on in his personal life. At present, he could be a liability to you."

Delta blinked. That was the worst possible thing for Miles right now. If Williams put him behind a desk, Miles would go nuts. "Sir, I have to say that I don't agree with that de—"

"I understand your reservations, Stevens, but I won't have an officer on the streets who isn't functioning at a hundred percent. Would you?"

"No, sir, I wouldn't. But even on his worst day, Miles is the best beat cop around."

Captain Williams nodded. "You're a good partner to him, Stevens. But unless he straightens up or takes some time off, I'm afraid I'll have to yank him."

"I understand." As Delta reached for the brass knob, she turned back to see Williams pushing down on a medical inhalant many asthmatics use. "Sir?"

Captain Williams held the medicine in his chest for a moment before exhaling. "Yes?"

"Miles has never put my life in jeopardy, and I hope you realize what a good cop he is. Putting him behind a desk, even for a week, would be a terrible waste."

"I'll be the judge of that, Stevens, but I appreciate your honesty."

As the glass door clicked behind her on her way out, Delta felt a ball of anger tighten in her stomach.

"You okay?" Connie asked, putting her *Math Monster* computer game away.

Delta nodded, still feeling the clamminess of her palms. "Does Captain Williams ever give you major creeps?"

Connie nodded. "Often."

Wiping her hands on her pants, Delta glanced over to the glass office and the burly man still sitting at his desk. "Me, too."

"Are you in trouble?"

Shaking her head, Delta gained a better grip of the firey ball burning in her. "Not me. Miles."

"Uh oh. Big trouble?"

Delta nodded. "Big trouble. And it's the last thing Miles needs right now."

"I don't suppose—"

"Not a chance. Williams never really listens to what we have to say. His mind was made up before I went in. I'm not even sure why he bothered talking to me at all."

For a moment, the two women looked at each other in silence, before Connie flicked her computer screen off.

"If he gets a burr up his royal ass, Miles is screwed."

Delta nodded. "I know."

"Fat Man might just take him off the streets, you know."

"I know," Delta replied as she stared through the glass at the Captain. In the darkness of his office as he hunched over papers, he reminded her of the Quasimodo high atop Notre Dame, hanging on with one hand and drool coming out of his mouth. "Con, do you ever wonder whose side he's really on?"

4

Tonight, Delta decided, she would get some answers from Miles. Up until now, she had been able to keep his drowsiness and restlessness to herself. But people were starting to take notice. And if so, it was time for her to pull her head out of the sand and deal with it. If he couldn't be honest with her, then maybe the Captain was right; maybe whatever he was doing was hazardous to her. Delta knew she couldn't go on protecting him indefinitely, especially when she didn't know what she was protecting him from. Signing out for a radio, Delta slid it casually into the container, adding even more weight to her overloaded belt.

"Ready?" Miles asked, dangling the keys in the air. This was his signal to her that he didn't want to drive.

"Sure." Taking the keys, Delta's gaze tried to penetrate through his eyes, as if it were possible for her to read some mysterious message.

"Come on, pardner," Miles drawled in his phony John Wayne accent, " Let's go get us some bad guys."

Carefully watching Miles's every movement, Delta cocked one eyebrow at him. He appeared in better spirits than he'd been in a long time. There was a lightness to his gait that set her at ease as he acted his usual cocky self.

"You must have had a nice day," Delta asked, starting the engine. The overhead clock read 6:05, but it was already beginning to get dark.

"As a matter-of-fact, I did. Jen and I went out to lunch and shopped around a bit until the kids came home from school. How about you?"

"I kicked around the house, watched some soaps, and did some laundry. Not the most thrilling of days."

For the next ten minutes they drove in silence, with only the squawking of the radio making a sound between them. Delta was turning the muster report over in her mind. This was their usual routine; a few bits of personal conversation before both ran through the day's reports. The Sarge had reported that there was an unusually high amount of tampered coke and crack on the street and much of it was beginning to filter into the schoolyards. A large shipment was believed to have landed in the area, but Vice had yet to locate the exact source. It appeared as if Vice was baffled by the amount of drugs flowing this time of year. Drug activity slowed in the winter as the cold kept people off the streets. But this year was dramatically different. Already, a number of busts had occurred in an area that normally had very little drug activity. This was an indication that there was a great deal more drugs on the street and that the pushers were forced to expand their dealing area. Delta winced, remembering the bust she and Miles had made on a kid who had been pushing drugs in Miles's kids' school. She thought he was going to kill that kid, he was so incensed.

"I also spent some time talking to Bassinger from Vice." Miles's voice interrupted Delta's thoughts.

"Oh?" She wished he'd get off this vice thing and concentrate on what they were being paid to do.

"He's not as closemouthed as the rest of those guys. I got some pretty interesting information from him."

Delta swallowed hard. What in the hell was he up to?

"Bassinger thinks the source of dope is coming from around our area and borders Patterson and McKlinton's beat."

Delta did not look at him, but stared straight ahead. The bar she'd gone to last night was in Patterson's beat; so was the Red Carpet. "Go on."

"This could be the one, Del."

Delta gripped the wheel harder. "Give it a rest, Miles. We'll get to Vice sooner or later."

"Sooner is my preference. Come on, Del, you know that you've got to make your own path in this business. You can't wait for the big busts to come to you. You have to create them."

Delta turned slowly. "Is that what you're doing? Creating a big bust?"

Miles said nothing.

"Miles, do you realize how close you are to being yanked off the streets?" Delta surprised herself with that bit of untethered honesty. And even more to her surprise, Miles nodded.

"I haven't been totally honest with you, Del."

"No shit."

"No, really. You know how badly I want to get to Vice."

Delta slowed and eyed a van driving suspiciously slow. "I hope you haven't done anything we're going to regret."

Miles shook his head. "Just the opposite. I'm just taking care of us, that's all."

Before Delta could respond, the dispatcher's voice crackled their number.

"S1012, what's your 20?"

Miles picked up the mike. "This is S1012. Our 20 is 8th and Dryden."

"You have a 416 at 1900 South Bronte, and see the lady."

"10-4." Miles laid the mike back on the arm.

A knot built up in Delta's stomach when she heard the address. 1900 South Bronte was next door to where she'd seen Miles last night. Whatever he was up to, he'd stopped hiding it from her.

"What's this all about?" she asked him as she turned left onto Bronte.

Miles rubbed his hands together like a greedy miser. "It's a bit premature to give you any of the details yet, but this is the info I've been waiting for."

Delta looked at him sideways. "Is that her?"

Miles jumped out of the car practically before she could stop it. When the car came to a stop in front of a "no parking" sign, Miles leaned back into the window and smiled. "This won't take but a second."

The knot grew tighter as she watched Miles approach a young woman in her mid-twenties wearing a red leather skirt and matching pumps. The long slender legs and silky blonde hair draped over her shoulders would normally have been admired by Delta. As a woman, Delta filed her beauty deep in her subconscious. As a cop, she took a snapshot with her eyes and filed it with a red flag. Whoever this woman was, she sent the alarms ringing in Delta's gut.

Miles spoke briefly with the woman, who handed him something, and then returned quickly to the patrol car. A second later, Delta pushed down the pedal and zoomed away.

"I think it's time you did some explaining, Miles." Delta's emotions were caught between anger, fear, and curiosity. This time, he would answer all of her questions, or she would return to the station and dump him at the door.

Before answering her, Miles picked up the mike and told the dispatcher they were all clear.

"Miles?"

Looking at Delta, Miles grinned. "Not yet. I'm on to something big. Really big. I don't have all of the pieces yet, so it would be too early to unfold it all to you. I have bits and pieces that are just now starting to come together. I want to tell you Del, and I will. As soon as I know what we're up against."

Delta suddenly jerked the car into a vacant parking lot and turned on him. "You've never kept a secret from me. Why now? Is it so dangerous that you would keep it from me? Or is it something else? Are you doing something you shouldn't be?"

Miles reached out and took one of Delta's hands. "I swear, that's not it. Right now, I'm just collecting pieces of a puzzle. I'm not about to jeopardize you or anyone else until I'm sure of what I have."

"What puzzle? What are you doing that is keeping you out on the streets at all hours of the night? Tell me. Give me something I can handle, but don't lock me out. Are you working undercover? Is that it?"

Miles shook his head. "Not officially. Look, Del, I really want to tell you—"

"Then do!"

"I can't. It's too soon to tell."

"I take it that woman is a part of it?" Delta's voice was heavy on the word "woman."

"You sound jealous," Miles responded, grinning.

"Maybe I am. You trust a hooker for God knows what, and you won't let your own partner in on it? Come on, Miles, how would you feel?"

"If you asked me to trust you Del, then that's what I'd do. I would know that no matter what you were doing, you had my safety first and foremost in mind because you care so much."

Delta turned her face away. She hated when he turned the tables and was right.

"Trust me."

Delta raised her face and looked hard into his steel blue eyes. "Would I really be in any danger if I knew what it was you were up to?"

Miles nodded. "Possibly. I'm not going to take that chance."

For a moment, the two officers locked eyes as they had done so often in the past when they fought to understand each other. Delta wanted to pry it out of him, but respected him too much to push him into a corner.

"Trust me?"

Delta acquiesced. "Of course. That goes without saying. When you're ready to tell me, I'll be ready to listen." Delta returned her hands to the steering wheel and dropped the gear into drive.

As she pulled out of the parking lot, Delta wondered how soon it would be before Williams put Miles on the desk.

5

Finishing off Val's chili, Delta leaned back in the booth and turned her radio up. Nothing could warm her in the frosty winters like Val's homemade chili.

"Did you see L.A. today?" Miles asked, pushing his burger away. "They're getting better. They might even make the playoffs."

Delta smiled. He was setting her up for this one. "Maybe a woman can own and run a professional football team afterall?"

Miles groaned. "Not that again. Come on Del, she got it by default."

"Yeah, it was default of her husband to die on her Miles, but you can't take what she's accomplished away because of how she got there. She's taken that team farther than he ever did." Delta waited for Miles to parley that into his own rhetorical assault, but instead, he was peering out the window watching a blue van coast by.

"What is it?"

"That's the third time that van has made a pass at this place."

"Got a number?"

Miles squinted. His night vision wasn't the greatest. "Yeah. Zebra Adam Peter, 914."

Delta hastily scratched it out on a napkin and called the number into dispatch. "Think they're casing?"

Miles shrugged. "Who knows? Let's wait for dispatch before leaving without dessert. It may be nothing."

Delta waited for the radio to crackle. Dispatch announced that the owner of the vehicle had no outstanding warrants, and that the vehicle registration appeared clean. Nothing out of the ordinary, yet Delta's stomach twitched as the van made its fourth swing by the restaurant.

"That's it," Miles grunted, tossing his napkin on the table. "Let's roll."

Jumping into the passenger side, Delta looked around the dark and nearly deserted streets. Many of the cops in the department hated their beat because of the macabre darkness sweeping through the many alleys and tiny one-way streets. But, not Delta. She loved it. There was something surrealistic about their beat. The night seemed darker and the cold, colder than other areas in the city, yet the night people who owned the city when the streets got dark, seemed to glow like the neon signs. They were the alter egos of the businessmen and women who tromped up and down the sidewalks during the day. And although the vampires of the night weren't wearing business suits and skirts, their safety was every bit as important to Delta as the businessmen and women's was to Officer Cornelius of the day shift.

"Where did it go?"

"South on East 14th, I think." Pushing the pedal to the floor, Miles burned out of the parking lot and down East 14th.

"This is S1012," Delta barked, her palms began sweating as she gripped the mike. Instinctively, her foot reached to the button on the floorboards and pressed it to release the shotgun. A slight click could be heard as the sturdy iron gate snapped open. Delta did not take the gun out, but rested in the fact that it was ready to go. "Vehicle is heading east on 14th past Johnson. Request backup unit between Poe and Woolf Street."

"S1012, is vehicle in sight?" came another voice from the radio.

Delta looked around. She felt the beating of her heart in her chest and temples. This adrenaline rush, this collaged moment dangling precariously between fact and fiction, was what so many cops lived for. It was the ten minutes of pants-shitting fear that made the other seven hours and fifty minutes worth doing. In that ten minutes, one experienced emotions that ran the gamut; from fear of losing one's life to fear that they might not get there in time. It was the reason they loved their job. But even reason warned her that a suspicious vehicle was as dangerous to them as an armed man.

"Negative," Delta responded, just before looking in her rearview mirror. "10-22. Suspect vehicle is now behind us."

Miles's eyes grew wide as he checked his own mirror. "I'll be damned."

"S1012, 10-9. Did you say behind you?"

Miles and Delta exchanged curious glances. "10-4."

As the radio came to life with various communications, Delta turned uneasily to Miles, who had slowed down considerably.

"I don't like it," Delta said, eyeing the van. "Wait for backup."

Miles shook his head. "Come on, Del. They obviously don't think we suspect them of anything or they wouldn't be behind us. Relax."

Before Delta could respond, the van made a quick U-turn and dashed down the street away from them.

Instantly, Miles jammed his foot on the accelerator, sending the patrol car rocketing forward and Delta back into her headrest. In the same instant, he turned the car to a perfect 180 degree turn and was quickly upon the speeding vehicle.

"This is S1012. Suspect vehicle is now heading west. Request backup."

The van made a sudden turn down Wilde Street. She did not like the way the people in the van appeared to be calling all the shots.

Flicking on the lamps and siren, Delta and Miles both reached for the spotlights on either side of the patrol car. Delta felt the ball of adrenaline gnawing on her stomach. Although she felt it was her job to protect the people of the night, she often found that she was protecting them from themselves. The city at night was much like a foaming ocean; turn your back to it, and it would devour you.

"Don't let him get to the freeway!" Delta shouted as they pulled up behind the van. Picking up the mike, she radioed dispatch of their location.

Positioning the spotlight on the two back doors of the van, Delta suddenly remembered her Sergeant in the Academy.

"Vans are the worst. They can see you, but you can't see them. They have the definite upper hand all the way. If the back door starts to open, you're shit outta luck if they're packing. That's their advantage. They know we're loaded, but we have to wait to see the weapon before blowing their fucking heads off. So be extremely cautious when pulling vans over. If you ever doubt your position of safety, stay in the car until every fucking advantage is yours. Whatever you do, don't get caught with your pants down."

Since that talk, Delta hated pulling over vans, hated knowing that they had the upper hand, and hated feeling vulnerable the moment she stepped away from the vehicle.

Watching the van slowly pull over, she turned to Miles and forced a grin.

"I know," he said, smiling back at her. "You hate vans. I'll take the lead."

Delta felt a pull in her stomach. The Sergeant's words echoed in her mind. "Let's wait for backup."

"Why?" Miles asked, reaching over and flipping off the siren and turning on the loud speaker. "They pulled over, didn't they? Come on, Del, this is the most excitement we've had all night."

Delta shifted her gaze to the van. It was very still and quiet outside and of the three street lamps towering over the road, only one was lit and it cast only a dim pallor on the concrete below it. To either side of them were old warehouses and a run-down railroad depot. Nothing outside moved. It was an eerie silence that lingered on her mind like rotten deviled egg lingered in the air.

"Besides, backup'll be here in a jiff. Relax." Without waiting for her indecision to transform, Miles opened his door, picked up the mike, and called to the driver.

"Put both hands out of the window so I can see them."

Delta opened her door and watched carefully as the passenger also put two slender arms out the window. Since

Miles had angled the car on them so that their right head-light was aiming at the middle of the van, Delta could not see the driver's side of the van. This did nothing to ease the growing apprehension inside her.

"Where in the hell is that back-up?" she thought angrily. For a second, she reached for the shotgun, but decided not to when the arms on her side started to move.

"Now reach your right hand out and open the door from the outside." Miles's voice crashed through the silence like thunder. Maybe that's what bothered her so. It was a silence stiller than dawn. Why weren't these people saying any-thing? Usually people responded when Miles or she gave simple orders. Most people were scared that the cops would accidentally shoot them.

This strange quiet was odd. The night was so silent, Delta heard the slow click of the driver's door as it opened.

"Hey man, couldya turn those lights down? You're blindin' me already." Delta heard the deep, resounding voice of the driver and knew it was a male. The passenger on her side did not move again.

"Let's just ID these punks and run 'em through," Miles said out of the corner of his mouth, not taking his eyes off the driver.

Delta nodded, still unmoving from behind her door. "Be careful."

She must have said those two words to Miles at least a thousand times since they became partners. It amused her in a strange sort of way, because that was exactly what her mother had always said to her as she headed off for school. And now, as a grown woman of twenty-eight, she echoed the same sentiments every time Miles left her side. It had become their standard trademark; one many of their col-leagues teased them about often.

Watching Miles maneuver around his door and toward the front of the police car, the bright beam from the spotlight shone across his broad shoulders. The light seemed to come alive as he entered it, and for a split second, appeared as an intense, dreamlike aura around his body.

In that fraction of a second, as the two back doors of the van loudly burst open, the world suddenly slowed to a sickening pace. Delta reached for the shotgun lazily reclining against the seat, but it was eternity before her fingers finally reached the cold metal barrel.

Grasping the shotgun, Delta yanked it to her, but in her gut she knew it was too late. She knew, by the crashing silence and too-still surroundings that the night had turned on them. As the doors noisily flew open, the gleaming barrel of a shotgun kicked toward the sky as the luminous orange blast reverberated through the air like the sound of a crashing avalanche. The flash from the barrel made the spotlights appear as two twenty watt bulbs, so bright and firey was the explosion. As the reel of film in life's camera ever so slowly clicked each frame away, Delta heard her own scream of pain and horror echo through the night as Miles's body was lifted like a broken marionette dangling by invisible guide wires.

In the harrowing moment that followed, his body was suspended for an instant, still captured by the aura of the spotlights, before being violently slammed to the cold pavement below.

"Miles!" Delta screamed, releasing the shotgun barrel she just managed to get a grip on and pulling out her own service revolver from its snug holster. By then, the van's doors had closed, and it was screeching out of the cover of the lights and down Wilde Street into the enveloping darkness.

"Oh my God, oh my God," Delta cried, jamming her revolver back in the holster as she scrambled around the front of the car. "Oh God, please, no, please."

Maneuvering around the grill of the car, Delta stopped at the feet of her battered and bloodied partner and screamed in anguish at the sightless eyes staring into the heavens.

"No!"

Rushing to his side, Delta knelt next to Miles and picked him up in her arms. "No, no, no," she cried, pulling his bleeding face to her chest. "Please, no."

She knew he was dead. Shotgun holes riddled his upper body, arms, neck, and face. Most of the left side of his jaw had been shot away, and his hair was already a thick mass of blood and bone. Only his eyes and forehead were unharmed. Hugging him tightly, Delta looked at the pavement and watched his life blood slowly drain onto the unyielding cement below.

"No, no, no," Delta murmured, feeling for a pulse. Struggling to maintain some tiny semblance of composure, Delta reached a bloodied hand across the seat for the mike. This wasn't happening, she told herself. It couldn't be happening to her Miles. Not Miles.

"Oh God," she said, swallowing hard as she gripped the slippery mike. "Control, Stevens. Get some control." Delta wiped her eyes, unknowing of the blood she wiped across her face. Inhaling deeply, Delta spoke hastily into the mike.

"This . . . this is . . . S1012. We have . . . a 406 . . . officer down. I repeat . . . officer down." The radio sputtered as officers radioed their locations and their estimated time of arrival. "Suspect vehicle . . . Zebra . . . Adam . . . Peter . . . 914. Heading . . . north . . . Wilde." Letting the mike slip from her hand, Delta gently picked Miles up in her arms and cradled him close to her.

"Not you, God . . . please, not you." Pulling Miles to her chest, unaware and unconcerned about the blood pouring from his wounds onto her uniform, Delta rocked back and forth stroking his wet, black hair. The night was so still, so quiet, it felt as if the end of time had come and left them behind. In the far distance of her fractured reality, Delta heard the radio voices yelling to her, asking her to answer, concerned for her welfare.

But she could not move. She would not move. Gently rocking and crying softly into Miles's wet hair, Delta wrestled with the fear and anguish ripping through her tormented soul. She felt the long, slow bleeding of a love that knew no bounds being violently and cruelly torn away from her. A long, hollow, echoing "No!" resounded through her spirit, as she struggled to balance herself on the fine line between sanity and insanity, between fact and a grotesque mockery of fiction. This was her worst fear and nightmare coming to life and dying in her arms.

Holding Miles's heavy body in her arms, Delta wept.

"Please don't leave me," Delta sobbed, cradling Miles close to her. "Please."

In another distance, she heard sirens blast their way to a scene that she knew had already come to its fateful conclusion. As the sirens pierced through the awesome stillness, Delta prayed a silent prayer to a God she wasn't sure was listening. She lived a thousand lifetimes as she sat on the side of the road rocking, crying, praying, cursing. In those thousand lifetimes, in those millions of grains of sand, Delta Stevens knew what it felt like for the world to come to a halt — leaving her totally, utterly alone.

In those lifetimes, Delta understood just how empty the soul can become.

6

Connie handed Delta's quivering hands a cup of hot tea and pulled up a chair for her. Wrapping both trembling hands around the cup, Delta was thankful for the warmth. It was the first real sensation she remembered feeling since she'd let go of the shotgun.

Around her, the squad room was abuzz as every available officer was put to task. Other than the heat from the mug, all that penetrated the gray, amorphous fuzz enveloping her mind was a dull murmur; like the busy hum of angry bees. Staring down into the tea, she thought of Miles's blood as it slowly, evenly spread across the pavement. Steam rose off it just like the steam rose off the hot tea. Quickly setting the cup down, Delta raced to the bathroom, barely in time to lower her head into the cold porcelain commode.

"Go ahead and get it all out, honey." Delta heard Connie's soothing voice before heaving a fourth time. Standing behind her, Connie was holding Delta's hair back and pressing a cool towel behind her neck.

After the last empty lurch toward the water, Delta sunk her head against the toilet seat, spent, dry, and exhausted. She was not even sure she had it in her to raise her head. Licking her lips, Delta swallowed back the burning sensation stinging her throat.

"Not Miles," she said hoarsely. "Not my partner."

Sitting next to her on the floor, Connie put her arms around Delta's jerking shoulders and pulled her closer.

"Oh God, Connie, it was . . . it was so . . . awful. He . . ."

"Shh," Connie whispered, stroking Delta's hair and rocking her. "Take deep breaths and try to relax."

Drawing in jerking breaths, Delta tried to get ahold of herself. It was so difficult being real, when reality seemed to distort itself right in front of her face. Even Connie's presence didn't feel right.

"Come on, hon. Let's get you out of these clothes." Connie carefully unbuttoned Delta's bloody shirt and slipped it off her trembling shoulders. The T-shirt underneath was also stained with Miles's blood, so Connie pulled that off Delta's body as well. Like a child, Delta allowed Connie to remove the rest of her clothes as the two women sat huddled together in the tiny green stall.

"I'll get your civvies, okay?" Slowly, gently, Connie untangled herself from Delta and returned briefly with Delta's jeans and sweatshirt.

"You okay to stand?"

Delta looked up at Connie, as if seeing her for the first time. The switch from a vacuum to a tangible existence was like a slap in the face. This really was happening to her. She would not wake up, as she had on a few occasions, to find herself in her own bed, drenched in sweat from some deathly nightmare; from a permanent photograph of some poor victim dancing spastically in her dreams.

Nodding, Delta stood long enough for Connie to slip the jeans on. When she finished, Delta slid back to the floor and leaned against the cold metal sides of the stall. She felt a hundred years old. Laying her face in her hands, Delta rubbed them back and forth across her face. Soon, the slow, jerking sobs returned, and she pulled her knees up to her chest and rocked back and forth. Connie sat cross-legged across from her and laid her hands on Delta's knees. For forty minutes, the two women remained in this position with neither saying a word. Finally, after all of the tears had poured freely and the realness of the catastrophe settled in for its lifelong stay, Delta tried to speak.

"I . . . have . . . to . . . report . . . to the . . . Captain . . ."

Connie nodded. "He can wait."

Delta shook her head. For the moment, her tears were dried up, and a new resolution started over her. She had to finish her duty. She had to get a grip on herself so she could be of some use in finding his killer. She certainly hadn't been of any use to Miles. Swallowing hard, forcing the jerking movements and unsynchronized breathing back into the strange netherworld from which it came, Delta let go of her knees and squeezed Connie's hand.

"No . . . he can't. I want to nail the bastard who did . . . this to him. You gotta help me . . . get my shit together." Throwing her arms around Connie, Delta hugged her tightly. "I've never hurt so much in my life. It was . . . worse than anyone could ever imagine."

"I know, honey."

"He was just laying there—"

"He was a good cop, Del."

Delta suddenly pulled away. "He was a great man, Connie, and deserved better than to die by the hand of a bunch of fucking low-life scumbags." Rising unsteadily to her feet, Delta took a step out of the stall before Connie reached out to stop her.

"You know what you're heading into, don't you?"

Delta swallowed and blinked hard to clear her eyes of the remaining tears. "I'm not doing Miles any good by falling apart at the seams. I'm a cop, goddammit."

Connie shook her head. "That's not what I mean. You know this is just the beginning of what will most likely be a very painful and long procedure for you. Give yourself a break here, Storm."

Delta did not respond. Even Connie's pet name for her didn't warm the hardening ice crystals surrounding her heart.

"Internal Affairs is going to ask you so many questions, you'll begin to question whether or not Miles was killed by a shotgun or a pellet pistol."

"I know." Delta's resolve did not waver.

Reaching out, Connie lightly held Delta's arm. "You go storming in there in this condition, and they'll bury you. Everything you say to them will come under close scrutiny. Think about it."

When Delta first came to patrol, and she and Connie hadn't even met yet, Connie nicknamed her Storm Stevens because of the way Delta rushed into everything. So great was her excitement of the job, Delta often dove headlong into trouble.

"They'll pick apart every little thing that you and Miles did, and at times, it will appear as if they're trying to prove that he simply fucked up."

"He didn't fuck up, Connie! That asshole blew his head off for no damn reason!" Tears she thought gone welled up in her eyes. "He didn't do anything wrong! He—" Suddenly, Delta heard herself and bowed her head. So many emotions bashed into each other inside her like pinballs, she didn't know how to feel. "Maybe you're right. Maybe I'm not ready."

Connie nodded. "No, but I think there's probably some other pertinent information that you may want to give to Captain Williams now. Do you think you can do that?"

Slowly raising her head, Delta inhaled deeply. Miles still needed her to be strong. For now, she could build a wall around the hurt and pain until she had completed her task. It was what he would have done. He would have been relentless in his pursuit in bringing down her killer. She had to do that for him now. Perhaps it was the only thing keeping her on her feet.

Nodding, Delta swallowed hard again. "Will you stay close to me? I swear Connie, this will be the hardest thing I've ever had to do."

Taking Delta's face in her hands, Connie shook her head. "I'm afraid, my friend, that you've already done that."

7

Captain Williams jumped out from behind his large desk and opened the door for Delta. The squadroom ceased humming as she made her way from the bathroom to his office. She felt all eyes on her, and if they were sympathetic eyes, she was too numb to notice.

"Please, St—Delta, have a seat." Closing the door behind her, the Captain also lowered the blinds to the window facing the squadroom. "Is there anything I can get you?"

"No, sir." Delta sat heavily in the chair and stared down at her hands folded neatly in her lap. She wanted to cry. She wanted to scream and yell and pull at her hair, but she was a professional, and a job still had to be done.

Sitting next to her, and not across the desk as he always had, the Captain placed a large hand on her shoulder. "I know that sorrys don't even begin to deal with the pain you're feeling, but I am sorry. Brookman was a hell of a good cop."

Delta's eyes moved from her still trembling hands and riveted on two beady brown ones looking down at her. There was a growing anger sprouting within her; anger at Miles, anger at the lack of backup, anger at herself, and anger at this man who had never taken the time to tell Miles how good he really was.

"Yes, sir, he was."

Captain Williams folded his own hands across his lap. "Are you sure you're feeling up to this? There's no hurry."

"Oh, yes there is. I want them caught and hanged for what they've done. And I won't rest until I see that done."

"I've got my best men on it already, Stevens. What I need from you is a clear head and as many details as possible. As much as I know you want to, you can't go off half-cocked looking for Brookman's killer. We work together on cases like these, you understand?"

Delta nodded, pushing her anger deep inside. "I'm alright, sir. I know what has to be done next, and I'm okay with that. Just don't treat me any differently because I'm a woman."

Captain Williams smiled. "Have I ever done that?" "No, sir. And I don't anticipate you doing it now."

"Alright. I'll tell you what we've got so far. If you have anything to add, or think of anything that we've forgotten, sing out. We've got a robin's egg blue van, possibly four door, carrying at least three people."

Delta nodded. She had been in such shock, she hadn't remembered giving this information when backup finally arrived. She barely remembered the ambulance arriving on the scene. Only when the paramedics were trying to pry Miles away from her, did she realize she was no longer alone.

"The van was apparently stolen less than an hour before you made the stop."

Delta rose in her chair. "When did you get the call?"

"Only minutes ago. Some guy was at a party and said that someone must have hot-wired his van."

"License Zebra Adam Peter—"

"914, yes."

"We haven't located the van?"

Captain Williams shook his head. "And we're checking the owner out as we speak."

"Think he's lying?"

Captain Williams shook his head. "He has about one hundred witnesses to corroborate his alibi. The van was stolen."

"Then it's still out there?"

"Yes. They've probably dumped it someplace, but we'll find it. We've got every available officer on the lookout."

Delta nodded. When a cop was killed, every precinct, every station, every officer would bust their collective humps to bring the murderer in.

Captain Williams moved behind his desk and used his asthma inhalant that was lying next to a report. "We also have a double-barreled shotgun, and something about the killer having strange eyes."

This comment puzzled Delta. "Strange eyes?"

Williams nodded. "That's what you said to one of the paramedics when they arrived on the scene."

Delta tried to remember, but couldn't even remember having spoken to the paramedic. It all happened in one huge red blur.

"Can you give us a sketch to go by?"

"I can try."

Pressing a chubby finger on the intercom button, Williams called for Jonesy, the police artist, who strode through the door only seconds later.

Jonesy sat next to Delta and smiled kindly. He was a mousy-looking guy, who probably got all A's in high school and college. But he was as good an artist as any.

"Take your time, Stevens. There's no reason to hurry. Whenever you want to start, just talk it through and ignore what I'm doing."

Delta forced her thoughts back. Both spotlights hit him the second the doors flew open. But had she really seen him? She remembered, vividly, how the gun glistened in the light. Did she even get a look at his face? Wasn't his face covered up? Delta shook her head. "I don't know, Captain. It happened so fast."

Jonesy gently touched Delta's leg. "That's natural, Stevens, to think you never saw his face. Most victims of violent crimes usually block that out for a time because it makes the crime that much more personal. For some, it takes days, even weeks, before their protective subconscious let's them remember. It'll come back to you."

"We don't have that kind of time," Delta growled, more at herself than at Jonesy.

Jonesy smiled and patted her leg before picking up his charcoal. "Then why don't you just tell me what you do remember seeing, and we'll work from there."

Delta inhaled. "The weapon. As clearly as if it was in this room."

"Good. Did you see his hands on it?"

Delta strained to remember. Something about his hands
. . . "Not his hands. I don't remember his hands. But I do
remember seeing something . . ." Closing her eyes, Delta
mentally allowed her eyes to travel up the barrel of the gun,
past his hands, until they rested on his shoulder. Something
was on his shoulder. "He had a tattoo on his shoulder."

"Excellent. Can you describe it?"

"It was partially covered up by a black, or was it blue,
tank top. He was wearing a dark colored tank top."

"Good. That's very good."

Delta looked to Captain Williams, who was smiling
slightly.

"And part of the tattoo was covered up by his shirt. It
could have been a snake, or a dragon, or anything. I was
really too far away to see."

"Could it have been a birthmark?" Jonesy offered.

Delta nodded. "I guess. It was big enough to see, but I
couldn't get any detail."

For the next thirty minutes, Jonesy went over color,
sizes, shading, shapes, everything that he could glean from
her words and fuzzy images.

At last, setting his board down, Jonesy patted her again.
"That's great, Stevens. You've done really well so far."

Delta forced a grin. "What next?"

"The most important part — his face."

Here, Delta drew a blank. She couldn't even come up
with the color of his hair. No matter how much Jonesy
prodded, Delta couldn't get a picture of it.

"I think that's enough for now," Williams said after
nearly an hour.

"No, Captain, I have to keep trying."

Moving his large girth from behind the desk, the Captain shooed Jonesy out the door and sat where Jonesy had
been sitting.

"Look, Stevens, how many seconds would you say you
had a clear view? Two, maybe three?"

Delta bowed her head and nodded. She felt like a failure.

"Given your pretty detailed account of the tattoo, odds are, you didn't even have the chance to look at his face. Anyone seeing a shotgun barrel poking out at their partner wouldn't see anything else either. So stop feeling as if you've blown it. You did everything you could do. And . . . you're still alive. That's the number one rule about this job. You know that."

"But—"

"No buts. I know how bad you want this bastard, but if you're going to be of any use to us, to Brookman, we need you to be fresh. "Go home, get some rest. Take a Jacuzzi, have a brandy, and hit the sack. I've been there, Stevens, and believe me, tomorrow is just the beginning. I.A. wants to see you first thing in the morning."

Delta stared down at her hands. The prospect of going home to an empty house compounded the fracture that ripped through her heart and poured a sour light on the loneliness she felt the moment Miles's life energy was snuffed from his body. Slowly, painfully, the tears burned her eyes once more.

"Now you go home and rest. Whatever you do, no matter how tempting it may be, don't get drunk. A hangover tomorrow will only make things worse."

"Yes, sir." Wiping her eyes with the back of her hand, Delta left the Captain's office and stepped into the vacuum of the outer offices. In an instant, Connie was at her side.

"You okay?"

Delta shook her head. "I don't think I'll ever be okay."

Guiding Delta to her desk, Connie gently pushed her into her chair. "Gina has the hot tub warmed up, the extra bed made, and clean pajamas next to the fire. Come home with me."

Sighing gratefully, Delta nodded. First Sandy left her and now Miles forever. God, she wondered, would she ever feel whole again?

8

The doors swung open as if violently kicked from within. Standing on the platform of the van, the huge, barechested man with ape-like arms wheeled the silver double-barreled shotgun into plain view. When he smiled, a silver tooth glistened like the shotgun. In an instant, the mouth of the gun belched a fireball, orange and yellow, as large as the sun itself, lifting Miles up and driving him hard into the ground.

"Miles!" Delta screamed, as the ape-man turned to her, still looking through the sights of the monster weapon. Indecision tormented her as she reached for her own service revolver. Resnapping her holster, Delta stared at the spectre before her as he smiled wickedly, and his eyes . . . what was wrong with his eyes?

"No!"

Sitting up in bed, finding her pajamas soaked through with nightmarish perspiration, Delta reached blindly for the light on the nightstand.

Connie and Gina appeared in her room just as the light went on.

"Storm, honey, are you okay?" Connie knelt at the bed and held Delta's sweaty hand.

"Oh God," Delta said, wiping her wet forehead.

"You dreamt about it, didn't you?"

Delta nodded, relieved she had not stayed home alone. "Only this nightmare made me remember something. Something was different about his eyes. I don't know what, but I remember them being . . . funny."

Was he wearing glasses?"

Delta shook her head. "I don't think so. They were just different."

Connie patted Delta's hand. "Good. As time goes by, you should be able to remember more and more."

Delta grabbed Connie's hand in both of hers. "Thanks for letting me stay here tonight. I don't think I could handle being alone."

"Don't be silly. I would never have let you go home alone. Stay here as long as you want."

Gina nodded. "You want to come sleep with us?"

Wiping the sweat off her forehead, Delta grinned sheepishly.

"She's serious, Del. We'll pack you right in between us so those nightmares can't possibly get to you."

Taking each of their hands, Delta squeezed them. "You two are too much. But if I'm ever going to get a handle on the nightmares, I might as well start now. Thanks, anyway"

"Well, if they get worse or you don't want to be alone, come into our room."

"I will. Good night."

As she watched Gina and Connie walk out of the bedroom, Delta pulled the covers up around her. She would get a handle on the nightmares, alright. It was reality she was worried about.

9

Captain Williams gave Delta the next two days off, although she spent one of them with Internal Affairs filing her report and answering a multitude of questions. They drilled her for hours, focusing on every minute detail imaginable. They kept coming back to why she had never drawn her weapon. To Delta, the questions were aimed at finding fault, and finger pointing, instead of at collecting enough information to go after the killer. Procedure was more important than outcome; tactical errors, if there were any, were their greatest focus; yes, they should have waited for backup, yes they could have pulled them over on a different, more well-lighted street, yes, they could have had their weapons drawn, and yes, she should have attempted to bring them down. But none of these answers would either bring Miles back nor would they aid in finding the mysterious blue van. She also hated being treated like a suspect instead of a victim. Her partner was dead. D-E-A-D. Instead of receiving sympathy, she and her actions would be used as an example of what not to do. Somewhere in the works, someone had forgotten to tell these guys that police work was people-oriented, not just facts and figures and product. Miles was just a sad statistic to these guys, and she knew it.

And she hated them for that.

When the barrage of questions finally ceased, Delta found herself preparing for a funeral she never anticipated going to.

"You hanging in there alright?" Connie asked, handing the mascara tube to Delta. In two days, Delta had been home just once, to feed the cats. She couldn't bear being alone. When she was alone, she felt a combination of cold numbness and searing pain.

"By a thread. I'll be fine until I see Jennifer and the kids." Delta had called over to the house on three different occasions, but all three times, Jennifer fell apart and her mother ended up taking the phone from her. Delta knew that seeing the three of them huddled together like fawns lost in the wilderness would rip open whatever was left of the fragmented emotions inside her. Then, her tears would be, not for Miles, not for her own sense of loss, but for them. They had lost a daddy and a husband. Surely that hurt more than losing a friend. Or maybe pain was an incomparable emotion that couldn't really be weighed against itself.

As their car rolled slowly past the church, Delta was struck by the number of blue, gray, and beige uniformed officers who were flooding into the small church.

"Death sure brings us out of the woodwork, doesn't it?" Gina put her arm around Delta and pulled her closer.

Delta inhaled slowly through her nose. The last three days felt like she was walking in someone else's nightmare and she couldn't escape. It was as if she would awaken at any moment, to find things back to normal. But she knew better. And, she knew worse.

"Ready?" Connie asked, turning off the engine and unstrapping her seat belt.

"It all feels so unreal."

Gina scooted off the seat and held the door open for Delta. "Not until you get back into the patrol car without Miles will this really hit you. You have a long grieving process ahead of you. This, I'm afraid to say, is really just the beginning."

"The beginning? Don't you mean, the end?"

Gina shook her head. Gina was the head nurse in one of the operating rooms at Mt. Glenn Hospital. She had a Bachelor's Degree in psychology, and when she spoke, which was not often, people tended to listen. Delta was listening hard to her now.

"No, I meant the beginning. Funerals signify the transition for the living, not, as some believe, for the dead. They are an indicator for us to acknowledge that we are sending the individual off to a better place and that our lives must begin again, without them. Miles's death is a time of transition for Jennifer, his children, his friends."

"So it's all about accepting a life devoid of his presence?" Gina nodded. "Maybe not this very second, but in there, you'll feel it working in you." Gina tapped Delta's chest. "You'll feel the transition in your spirit as you learn that."

Delta sighed. She didn't feel like a new beginning.

"There's Jennifer," Connie said, pointing. "She looks awful."

Delta took a deep breath and approached her. For long, tender, painful moments, the two women stood, not knowing what to say to ease the other's pain, yet saying all that needed or could be said. A river of sorrow seemed to flow between them, yet there was a small comfort in knowing that they weren't truly alone in their pain. Finally, Delta looked into Jennifer's sad, gray eyes, and saw the same fear, same sense of loss, only deeper, more gaping; the river was much larger for Jennifer than Delta could even imagine.

Wrapping her arms around Jennifer, Delta held her. The moment they touched, the river broke free and Jennifer began sobbing.

Holding Jennifer close to her, Delta asked the father if there was someplace they could go to be alone. After showing them to his chambers, Delta sat down, still holding Jennifer, and said nothing.

After a few minutes of heart-wrenching crying that wracked her body with violent jerks, Jennifer slowly took a tissue out of her purse and wiped her eyes. "I . . . I suppose you know . . . I haven't been willing to talk to anyone from the station."

Delta only nodded.

"You know why, too. All they would have done was feed me a line of shit. They always think we wives are too weak to handle the truth. But we're the ones who see our husbands break down after a child has been molested or murdered. I was the one who held Miles while he cried after that horrible child abuse at the preschool. I may not have been there to see the things he did, but I felt what seeing them did to him. I'm stronger than that, Delta. You know it, too."

Delta nodded again.

"And I couldn't talk to you because . . . because it hurt so much. You were there. You held him as he died. It was too unbearable to be that close to his death."

"I understand. Really."

"And I knew, I know, that you will tell me the truth. You won't hide anything from me, even if it hurts."

Delta reached for Jennifer's hand and held it in her own. They were chilled.

"I understand that you saw the whole thing."

Delta winced and then nodded once.

"I just want to know . . ." Jennifer struggled to maintain control. "Did he suffer?"

Squeezing Jennifer's hand, Delta shook her head. "No, Jen, he didn't. It all happened so fast."

Jennifer fell back into the brown leather chair. "Thank the Lord. I was so afraid—"

"We did everything by the numbers, Jen. He wasn't careless, he didn't screw up. No matter what the final investigation report says, you must believe that."

Jennifer nodded. "I know that. He would never endanger your life by heroics or stupid antics." Jennifer let out a deep sigh. She looked twenty years older than her thirty-four years. Her eyes were sunken and dark, and wrinkles around her eyes and mouth had formed overnight. Delta knew from experience she hadn't slept much.

Leaning over, Jennifer touched Delta's knee. "How are you doing? It must have been awful."

"I'm hanging in there. You don't lose a friend like Miles without it tearing a grand canyon-size hole in your heart." Delta sighed loudly. "The nightmares are the worst."

"I can't imagine what it must have been like for you."

For a moment, Delta drifted off to the recurring image plaguing her. It was Miles alive, laughing, vibrant one moment, and violently ripped away from her the next.

"Delta, I know how much you meant to Miles. He talked about you all the time." Jennifer grinned. "As fond of you as he was, if I didn't know you were a lesbian, I'd have thought he was having an affair."

Delta grinned back. Her sexuality had been a topic of conversation in the patrol car on many occasions, and Delta remembered, years ago, when Miles shared with her how relieved Jennifer was to know that his partner was a lesbian.

Before Delta could reply, the father poked his head through the door. "Excuse me, Mrs. Brookman, but I'm afraid we need to get started."

"Thank you, father." Turning back to Delta as she stood, Jennifer looked her square in the face. "He wasn't, was he?"

For a second, Delta was unsure of the question. "What? Having an affair?"

Jennifer nodded. "Or something like that."

Two months ago, Delta would have been taken aback by such a question from Jennifer, but she remembered her own questions just days ago. "No, Jen, he wasn't. And I honestly believe he would have confided in me if he had. We didn't have too many secrets."

Jennifer wiped her face with the tissue before gazing deeply into Delta's eyes. "I believe you," she said, bowing her head as if ashamed that she could ask such a question. "I guess I just needed to hear it from you."

Delta followed Jennifer out the door and took her seat next to the children. They too, looked older than their years. In all of her life, Delta never felt more pain than she did when she looked down at the two innocent faces staring out at her. They did not understand death. They did not understand what would possess someone to do what had been done to their father. Their innocence, their fragility, drove the pain deeper into Delta's soul.

As the father opened to a church that was wall-to-wall with blue uniforms, Delta glanced around at the mournful faces. She had worked with many of the people there, and many of the married officers had their wives sitting closely to them, lest the angel of death choose them next time. There were lawyers, doctors, merchants from their beat, and people who could have been Miles's childhood friends. All these people, most of whom had never met, all shared a tiny piece of the memory of Miles Brookman. If they had nothing else in common, they had all known a very special person.

As Delta started to turn back around, her eyes stayed glued to the face of a pretty young woman sitting in the back pew. Eyes transfixed on a woman who appeared to be in her mid-twenties, Delta scanned her memory bank for the information on this woman. With beautiful, blonde hair flowing over her right shoulder, Delta zeroed in on the red lipstick. Red lipstick. The red brought the red pumps and leather skirt to her memory. This was the woman Miles had stopped to see that evening.

Wheeling back around, Delta's palms began to sweat. What was a hooker doing at a cop's funeral? And what was this particular hooker doing here now? Did she know something about Miles's activities. Oh God, Delta thought, how could she sit through the whole funeral, wondering whether or not that woman would slip through her fingers? What would Miles or Jennifer think if she suddenly raced through the church chasing after a woman?

Miles, she thought wryly, would say she was a damn good cop.

Turning back around, the woman locked eyes with Delta. For a moment, neither moved. Suddenly, adeptly, the woman slid off the pew and scooted out the door. A fraction of a second later, Delta tore down the center aisle in pursuit.

Two steps from the door, six steps away from catching her, an extremely large gentleman known to all as "Bear" leapt out in front of Delta and stopped her.

"Delta, it's gonna be okay," Bear said soothingly, taking Delta into his arms and hugging her tenderly. "We understand how hard this must be on you."

Delta looked up at the hulking man taking up most of the aisle and shook her head. The church had grown extremely quiet in the wake of her mad, unexplained dash.

"Miles would want you to stay," Bear whispered. Bear was one of Miles's best friends. He was a California Highway Patrolman who had gone to the Academy with Miles and had come as backup for Miles a couple of times just because he cared. The two men had a bond Delta always admired, and even now, Bear was thinking about what Miles would want.

But Delta knew better.

Thinking of the only thing that could get him out of her way, Delta stood on her tiptoes and whispered, "I think I'm going to puke."

Immediately, Bear stepped aside, allowing Delta to brush past him and go through the door.

Once outside, she looked up and down the street, but the beautiful blonde with the red lipstick was gone.

Looking into the sky, Delta sighed. "Okay Miles, she beat me this time, but I swear to God, I'm going to find out the secret you've been hiding from us all. And if I have to, I'm going to twist it out of your little friend in red."

10

"Have you been back to work?" Jennifer asked, handing Delta a cup of coffee.

"I'm on light duty until Internal Affairs is finished with their investigation. God, is it boring." Delta tried not looking at the box on the floor that contained most of Miles's police gear. Jennifer had called her earlier that morning saying that she had found some peculiar things in Miles's safety deposit box. Delta wasted no time in coming over, but the small box filled with items that were once so important to Miles, struck a melancholic chord deep within her.

"Miles used to say that Internal Affairs was like the keystone cops; they couldn't tell the difference between their ass and a hole in the ground."

Delta smiled. She'd heard him say that a number of times.

"How is the investigation going?"

Delta shrugged. "Same old stuff. I wish someone would answer my questions."

"What questions are those?"

Shaking her head, Delta leaned on her left elbow. "Where the hell was our backup? We requested backup nearly two full minutes before we made the stop. How long did they want us to wait?" Delta rubbed her tired eyes. She had asked that question nearly a hundred times.

"Miles didn't want to wait, did he?"

Jennifer knew her husband well.

"No, Jen, he didn't. They were very late in backing us up. If I were I.A., I'd be asking our backup a whole lot more questions."

Jennifer nodded. Her gray eyes were soft and caring. "I want you to know I don't blame you. I know how much you loved him, and I know you would never have let anything happen to him if you could have prevented it."

Delta's eyes welled-up. God, how she had needed someone to say that to her. Instantly, half her burden of self-imposed guilt lifted from her drooping shoulders. "Thank you. So often I wonder about all of the what-ifs." Delta looked down at her hands. She felt tired and old.

"Doing that will only make you crazy."

"Sometimes, Jen, I feel like I'm already there."

Jen leaned closer to Delta. "There's something more, isn't there?"

Delta looked up from her hands and into Jennifer's face. She didn't wish to burden a woman who had lost the most important part of her life. "Sort of. I don't have a handle on anything concrete yet, but when I do, I'll let you know."

Turning from Delta, Jennifer pulled a small spiral-bound notebook out of the box on the floor. "Maybe this will help. When I went to get his off-duty weapon, I found this tucked inside a manilla envelope."

Taking the pad from her, Delta opened it up and found a list of a series of numbers. The first number read, 7336412201. Delta stared at the list of about thirty numbers for a long time.

"What do they mean?"

Delta shrugged. "Beats me. I've never seen them before."

"Do you think that Miles was in some kind of trouble?"

Delta lowered the pad and cocked her head. "What makes you ask that?"

Looking out the window at the soft rain, Jennifer sighed. "He'd been acting so strange lately."

"Strange?"

"You know, not coming home until well after his shift, leaving really early for work. That's . . . that's why I asked you what I did at the funeral."

"Did you ever confront him on it?"

"I did ask why he was getting home so late. All he would ever say was that this was his tickct to bigger and better things."

Delta nodded. He had said that to her as well. Whatever he had been doing, the generic story remained the same for both of them.

"I wish I knew what to say, Jen."

"You don't have to say anything. You being here is enough. The kids ask about you often." Jennifer reached out and laid her hand on Delta's leg. "I don't think it's quite hit them that daddy isn't coming home anymore."

Delta gently laid her hand on top of Jennifer's. They were still cold. "Is there anything I can do?"

Jennifer pushed the manilla envelope closer to Delta. "Finish what he started. He would want that."

Delta looked down at the worn envelope.

"There's one more thing I'd like you to have." Reaching into the box, Jennifer pulled out a small package wrapped in cotton and handed it to Delta.

Carefully unwrapping it, Delta looked down at Miles's shiny, silver shield. "But I thought—"

Jennifer shook her head. "I only told them that I was burying him with it on. I know that he would have wanted you to have it, Del."

Looking down at the glittering badge, Delta could almost feel Miles's presence.

Wiping the tear from her eye, Delta looked up at Jennifer through blurry eyes. "Thank you, Jen. I'll treasure it forever." Slipping it into her pocket, Delta grabbed the envelope and headed for the door.

"If there's anything I can do . . . anything."

Jennifer hugged her tightly before opening the door. "Find who killed my husband, Delta. If anyone can do that, you can."

"I'll give it my best. I can promise you that much."

11

Staring out the window of the bar, neon beer names flickered on and off, Delta looked at their reflection in the crystal of her watch. This was the second night she'd come downtown hoping to see some sign of the red leather skirt and pumps. The rain had slowed to a fine mist, and the city's nightlife bloomed. Tonight was the night, Delta told herself, that she would catch that woman and find out everything she could.

Three hours later, she was right.

After waiting and watching, Delta saw the blonde on the corner of the street outside. Jumping off her barstool, Delta raced through the front door and jammed across the street, dodging two cars at the intersection.

Delta was on her before the woman had a chance to move.

"Let go of me," the hooker cried, hitting Delta with her purse.

Delta grabbed her wrist to keep her from bolting down the street. "Please, listen!" Delta yelled above the noise of the city. "Please, I'm not going to hurt you. I need some information, that's all."

The hooker struggled to break Delta's grip on her wrist. "I don't have any. Let go of me."

Delta released her arm and took a step away. "You know I'm a cop, don't you?"

The woman straightened her dress and looked the other way.

Delta stepped closer. "You do know who I am." It was not a question.

The woman rubbed her wrists, but did not return Delta's penetrating gaze.

"And you knew my partner as well." Delta stepped even closer. The woman was an inch or so taller than Delta, but she seemed to shrink from Delta's strong presence.

"I don't have to talk to you," the woman said, showing a perfect row of bright teeth. "You have no right to just stop me and ask questions."

Delta realized the interrogative nature of her posture and backed off. "I'm sorry. I'm not looking for any trouble. It's just that I saw you at my partner's funeral . . . I'm sorry if I hurt your wrist."

The blonde stopped rubbing her wrist and looked at Delta coolly. "You're not going to bust me?"

"No. I swear. I told you, I saw you at the funeral, and I'm looking for some answers, that's all. I thought—"

"That I was banging your partner? What makes you think I would even give you that kind of information?"

Delta shrugged and backed away, feeling dazed and confused. She wasn't even sure she wanted to hear this. "Look, I'm terribly sorry for chasing you out of the funeral the other day and for grabbing you just now. I think, maybe I need a break. I'm . . . really sorry." Jamming her hands in her pockets, Delta turned and walked away. She had never felt so lost in her life.

"Delta, wait!" Catching up to her, the woman lightly touched her arm.

Delta turned to face her. She was not wearing her red lipstick. "You do know me."

"Well, sort of. It's a long story."

"I've got time." Delta wanted to laugh. Miles probably thought that very thing. "And I'll pay for it."

The woman straightened her dress and looked Delta in the eye. "Damn right you will."

"How much?"

The woman pretended to think it over. "Hmm. How about a dollar?"

Delta cocked her head. "A dollar?"

"Or a cup of coffee and a danish. Whichever is more expensive."

Delta didn't know if she was kidding or not. "I'd say coffee and a danish would be more expensive, wouldn't you?"

A wry smile appeared on the woman's smooth face. "I wouldn't know. You cops spend all your time at Winchell's Donut Shop. You tell me."

Delta hesitated a moment. "You're serious?"

"You want to talk or don't you? Buy me a cup of coffee and we can talk."

Delta did not move. She didn't know what to say.

Suddenly, the woman's expression changed. "Miles was a great guy. You don't have to be a cop to know that. I imagine the last few days have been rough on you."

Delta nodded. Rough wasn't even close. "The hardest days of my life. Look, I'm really sorry about the other day. It's just—"

"Forget it," the woman interrupted, waving the thought off with one of her manicured hands. "Other than the broken heel of my shoe, no harm done."

"A good friend of mine calls me Storm because—"

"Because you used to storm all over the place? I know . . . Miles told me." Her smile widened. "Seems to me your old habits have resurfaced."

Reaching her hand out, more in gratitude than formality, Delta smiled. "Let's start over. You seem to have the advantage. You know who I am, but I don't know who you are."

The blonde smiled, knowingly. "My name is Megan," she said, accepting Delta's hand firmly in her own. "You can call me Ms. Osbourne."

Delta's eyebrows raised.

"I'm only kidding. Geez, you cops can be so stuffy."

"Well, Ms. Osbourne, if you'll be so kind as to call us a cab, I'll gladly pay the fare."

"You're a fast learn, Officer Stevens."

Watching Megan Osbourne confidently hail a cab, Delta smiled. She liked her already.

12

Her eyes were a deep, sapphire blue, twinkling now and then when the light hit them at just the right angle. She was prettier than Delta remembered, and far more gracious and well-spoken than most hookers Delta had run into. She liked that Megan wasn't about to let anyone stereotype her into the Hollywood idea of a prostitute. But then, after spending a few minutes with Megan Osbourne, it was easy to see why she wouldn't.

After ordering two cups of coffee and some pie, Megan smiled gently into Delta's face. "I can tell that you're sitting there trying to be polite and contain yourself, but you're jumping out of your skin with questions. Why don't you just go ahead and ask me?"

Delta let a slow grin creep over her face. "How could you tell?"

"Darlin', it's my business to know people. To watch them."

"Is that what you were doing for Miles?" Delta saw her opening and dove for it.

"Sort of."

"Sort of?"

"Yeah. See, lots of our girls service your guys in blue. At first, Miles wanted me to keep track of who was coming and going — if you'll excuse the pun."

Delta rested her chin on her hands. Megan had perfect rows of pearl-white teeth. "For what purpose?"

"I don't know. Does this have anything to do with his death?"

Delta fidgeted. She was, afterall, on the opposite side of the coin where the law was concerned. "What makes you ask that?"

Megan shrugged. Clearly, two could play this game.

Before Delta could ask another question, Megan leaned over the table. "Miles trusted me."

Delta nodded. "Yes, he did. What I don't understand, if you'll excuse me for asking, is why?"

"As hard as it may seem, Miles and I were very good friends."

"I don't doubt that you were. It's just—"

"What? That you thought you knew everything about him, and suddenly, there's a prostitute in the picture?"

"Something like that."

Megan leaned against the back of the booth and draped one arm over the back. "As I'm sure you know, Miles didn't think prostitutes are the scum of the earth. We had a very nice friendship. That was all."

Delta inhaled deeply and clasped her hands together. "I believe you."

Megan leaned forward, her eyes now a shade of ice blue. "You better. Miles told me you had exceptional intuitive powers. Look me in the eye, Delta Stevens, and tell me what your gut tells you now."

Delta leaned forward and did as Megan asked. There was an honesty about Megan that permeated the air around her. Clearly, this was a no-bullshit kind of woman.

"Well?"

Backing away from the intense blue of her eyes, Delta nodded. "Will you help me?"

Megan didn't move and was halfway across the table. "What is it you need?"

"You know what I want. Miles was investigating something big, and you know what it was."

"You base this on one look at the two of us?"

Delta nodded. "You handed him something. You don't have to work in Vice to know that it's usually the other way around."

Megan ran her hand through her hair. "True."

Delta drew a breath in through her teeth. "It's possible that's why he was killed."

Megan's eyes narrowed. "Then you do think the two are connected."

"I don't have a shred of evidence one way or the other. All I know is, my partner was doing something surreptitiously one minute and is dead the next. Maybe I'm grasping at straws, but he was up to something, and it involved you. You tell me what to believe."

"I don't know." Megan slowly opened her purse and pulled out a matchbook. "I was going to leave this at the funeral, but I thought maybe I should keep it." Tossing it on the table, she sighed. "I can honestly tell you that I don't know what Miles was looking for."

Delta picked up the matchbook and looked inside. On the inside of the cover was a list of numbers, different from the ones Jennifer found on the notepad; shorter. Next to each number was another number, two or three numbers in length.

"What's this?"

"I kept track of the patrol car numbers when they came by and listed whether or not they visited one of the girls. Miles has four more."

"Four more matchbooks?"

Megan nodded. "Yes."

Delta turned the matchbook over in her hand. "Did he tell you why he wanted this information?"

"Not really. One time, he said something about the Red Carpet being a rat's nest, but that was about it. All I know is, I gave him the matchbooks and he tossed me fifty; which, by the way, I usually tossed right back. I make more than Miles ever did."

Delta reached for her wallet, but Megan put out a hand to stop her. "I don't want your money. I want to help."

Delta looked up from Megan's neatly polished hand resting firmly on hers. There was a warmth and a softness to those blue eyes that caught Delta off-guard.

"I did it as a favor."

Delta grinned. "A favor? Were you sweet on him?"

Megan tossed her head back and laughed. "I suppose at one time I might have been. One time a very long time ago."

Delta did not move her eyes from Megan's.

"Miles and I go way back. We were childhood friends from long, long ago."

Delta sat up. "No kidding?"

"We went all through school together until I dropped out of high school when I was sixteen. We weren't best friends or anything like that, but we grew up in the same neighborhood. We walked to grammar school together almost every day. Once we got to high school, he discovered sports and I discovered sex." This made Megan laugh to herself. "Anyway, to make a short story long, Miles and his first partner, a real dick, mind you, were rounding up the girls one night, and there I was. He didn't know what to say."

Delta was mesmerized by both the story she had never heard and the eyes that danced when she spoke.

"Did he haul you in?"

Still smiling, Megan shook her head. "No. We went for coffee when he finished work and caught up on each other's lives. We got into a great discussion about victimless crimes. I must have won the argument because as far as I know, he hasn't arrested any of us since."

Delta grinned. She had wondered where Miles got his liberal attitude on the oldest profession.

"And after that?"

The smile faded from Megan's lips. "He came to see me late one morning after his shift. It was a few days after you guys busted that pusher at his kids' grammar school. I think that sent Miles toward the edge. He came to me wanting to know more. He wondered if I could get a handle on where the drugs were coming from, and said he wanted whoever it was that was putting it back out on the street. He wanted them bad."

"There has been more dope on the street lately."

Megan nodded. "Hell yes. Lots, cut, and bad. Even the bigger pushers don't know where it's coming from. I did a lot of asking around for Miles, but came up with nothing.

Wherever these drugs are coming from, nobody on the street knows."

"That's odd."

"It's weird. I have a client who's a family member, and even he said that it isn't their stuff. I thought for sure it was mob-related. He was very offended when I inquired. This shit is apparently being cut with some pretty rank shit. The family prides itself in good cuts."

This made Delta smile. Megan brought the world of crime into a unique and colorful light. "What does Miles's preoccupation with street drugs and patrol car numbers have in common? A lot of cops have their own hookers."

Megan winced. "We prefer the term escorts, or, if you must, prostitutes. Hooker to us is like pig to you."

Delta blushed. "I'm sorry. Cop jargon."

Megan grinned. "I understand. Miles never could get it either."

Delta waited for the waitress to deliver the coffee before saying anything. "So you took notes about patrol car numbers?"

Megan nodded. "And anything else I had time to notice, such as, how long they stayed at the hotel. I wasn't real thorough because I had my own job to do."

"And you say that Miles has four more?"

"I'm telling you, those cop cars came by on a regular basis."

"Did you," Delta hesitated, not sure if she was overstepping her bounds. "Did you . . . service any of these guys?"

Megan shook her head and smiled. "I don't do cops."

"Oh."

Reaching across the table, Megan touched Delta's wrist. "Because they want it for free. I have a hard time with giving things away."

"Aren't you afraid they'll bust you if you don't?"

The smile suddenly vanished from Megan's face. "Now I am. I wasn't afraid before because I had Miles."

Sipping her coffee, Delta did not take her eyes off Megan's. The genuine sadness at her loss was evident.

"Anyway," Megan started, sweeping her hand through the air as if she was brushing the sadness away, "I recorded recurring patterns or anything out of the ordinary."

"And you don't know what he was looking for?"

"I haven't a clue. Usually, when Miles and I would meet, we talked about our personal lives."

Delta leaned back and shook her head. She thought she knew everything there was about Miles.

"I would have come to you sooner or later with this."

"Why?"

Megan looked away for a moment before answering. "He told me a lot about you. And if it was so important to him, I figured you would want it."

Delta picked the matchbook off the table and dropped it in her pocket. "That was an excellent read."

Brushing her silky hair casually over her shoulders, Megan leaned over the table. Delta could smell the slight spiciness of her OPIUM perfume as it mixed gingerly with the hot aroma of Megan's cappuccino.

"I told you — it's my business to know people." Megan motioned to the waitress for another cappuccino.

Again, Delta hesitated as she tried to find the best words to form her next sentence. "Would it be terribly offensive if I told you that you're not like any other hoo—prostitute I've ever met?"

The whites of Megan's teeth shined in the night. "I should hope not. Why would that be offensive?"

Feeling the heat rise in her face, Delta fidgeted with her spoon. "Well . . . it's just that you sound extremely intelligent and appear resourceful. I don't understand why you do what you do."

"Ah." Megan leaned back and ran her fingers through her hair. "I'm not your every day variety prostitute, am I?"

Delta swallowed loudly. "Am I out of line here?"

Megan tossed her head back and laughed. "Of course not. I must admit that I'm not at all like most of the girls who do it because they're hooked on drugs, have a child to

support, or have a man. Believe it or not, I'm in my second
year at the university."

Delta leaned forward, coming out of the chair. "Really?
That's wonderful. What's your major?"

Grinning, Megan finished her first cappuccino as the
waitress brought the second. "What else? Business. I woke
up one morning wondering what I was going to do when I
was forty or fifty, and I got scared to death. The retirement
package in this line of business isn't spectacular."

Still hanging over half of the table, Delta asked, "So how
did you get started?"

"Like so many other young, dreamy-eyed girls out of
high school, I came to the big city to make my fame and
fortune. I actually came out here to be a hand model."

Delta had been noticing her hands ever since they
arrived at the coffee shop. Her fingers were long and perfectly proportioned, and her painted nails were brightly
colored talons.

"Needless to say, that never happened and my money
had run out. A friend of mine showed me the ropes until I
could make enough money to get a portfolio done, pay for
bus fare to agents, and keep some food in my stomach. Next
thing I knew, I was ten years older and still doing it. Can't
beat the money, that's for sure."

Delta leaned further onto the table, enchanted by the
clear eyes and expressive mouth. She was beautiful and
alarmingly charming, with a voice of honey. "But doesn't it
ever bother you?"

"Morally?"

"Something like that."

Megan smiled, and the start of crows feet showed up on
the corner of her eyes. "I sell a service, Delta. It just happens
that my body is the product men buy. When I was younger,
I didn't get hung up on the morality of it all. It kept me fed
and clothed. It was good money. It still is."

"And when you get your degree?"

"Then I'm out of here. I've been on my back long enough.
In three more years, I'll be done, and I can look forward to

starting a different kind of life. That's what really excites me, the newness of a day job. To do something with my degree will be the accomplishment of my life."

Delta couldn't help smiling. Megan mesmerized her. "From what I've seen, you'll succeed."

Megan smiled appreciatingly at the compliment. "So, maybe this cop's preconceived notions can be reconceived?"

Delta nodded. "Most definitely."

"I'm glad. But then, I'm not surprised. The way he described you, I knew you wouldn't be one of those hard-nosed cops who see everything in black and white." Running her index finger around the rim of her mug, Megan's voice softened. "He was crazy about you, you know. Talked about you all the time."

"Really?" a warm blush blossomed around Delta's cheeks.

"Oh yes. He thought so highly of you and spoke with such love and admiration, I asked him if he was in love with you."

Delta gulped audibly. Megan's candor was unsettling.

"He said, in a way, he was. He loved your strength, your compassion, and he loved how you followed your convictions. He said you were the best cop he'd ever worked with and that you were his best friend."

Delta did not know what to say. Here, she thought she knew him so well, and now she finds out that he spoke about her to someone she didn't even know existed until a few days ago. Did they have more secrets between them than she knew? Perhaps she did not know him as well as she thought.

"But you weren't in love with him either, were you?"

Leaning away from the intensity of her question, Delta wondered how the tables had been turned. Afterall, wasn't she supposed to be asking the questions?

Megan waved off Delta's non-answer. "That's okay. The way I figured it, you never fell in love with him because you couldn't."

Delta's eyebrows shot up again.

Grinning softly, Megan leaned forward again. This time, she spoke barely above a whisper. "Miles was an incredibly wonderful man. He was handsome, sensitive, warm, bright, and excellent company; a rare combination in most men. My colleagues would have slept with him for nothing. You, on the other hand, are a single woman devoted to your job and your partner. Nine out of ten women in your shoes would surely have fallen in love with him; unless, of course, she was that one-in-ten who was a lesbian."

The sweat on Delta's palms immediately broke the surface. Suddenly, she felt naked in front of this woman, whose eyes seemed to pierce her very soul. It was disconcerting having someone be able to read her so well when they had never met before.

"He told you."

Reaching to one of Delta'a hands, Megan lightly touched it. "He didn't mean to. Actually, he only alluded to it. One night, he made the comment that he wished you and I could meet because, let's see, how did he put it? *Del would find you really attractive.* He worried that you didn't go out enough."

Delta shook her head. "I got dumped a few months ago, and I haven't made much of an effort to make myself available."

Megan's eyes softened. "So you threw yourself into your work."

"Miles tell you that?"

"It's a guess."

This brought a slight grin to Delta's face. She was enjoying their conversation more than she intended. For some reason, she was very comfortable with Megan; as if they had known each other in another place, another time.

"Well, it's a good guess. But enough about me. What about you? Your job must make it difficult to have a relationship."

Finishing the last of her pie, Megan wiped her hands on her napkin before answering. "Difficult? Try impossible. I've been with men and women who, for some reason, turn into instant sponges when they get together with me. Then there's been the occasional sugar daddy type who wants to *take me away from it all."*

"That's not so bad."

"I don't want charity, Delta. I've made my own way so far, and that's exactly what I'm going to continue to do. It's the only way I know of. Miles was the only man who understood that."

"Were you in love with him?"

Megan shook her head. "I was in love with the friendship. It was so refreshing to talk to a man whose last priority at that moment was sex. Being with him always reminded me that there were good men out there with warm hearts and sensitive thoughts. I'll miss that friendship."

This time, Delta reached across to squeeze Megan's hand. "I know how you feel. There's a gaping hole where he used to be."

Megan nodded and turned her hand over so that she was now holding Delta's hand. "You're every bit as special as Miles said you were. I hope you've enjoyed our talk as much as I have."

Delta nodded, thought about pulling her hand away, then decided against it. There was something comforting and warm about holding Megan's beautiful hand. It was as if it supplied her spirit with tenderness she was so desperately needing.

"I have. Look, I know this may sound strange and all, I mean, we've just met and I'm not trying to replace Miles or anything, but—"

Megan smiled her largest smile of the night. "Yes, you can have my number, but only if you do the same. If you pull that cop confidentiality shit on me, forget it. It worked with Miles because the trust went both ways."

"I don't trust too many people, "Delta said, surprised by her own candor.

"Well, Delta Stevens, you can trust me."

Squeezing Megan's hand, Delta slowly pulled hers out of Megan's grasp so she could write down her phone number. Sighing heavily, Delta was thankful for Megan's honesty and was grateful she hadn't offended her by asking for her number. The last thing she wanted to do was to scare Megan off.

As Megan handed Delta her phone number, Delta laughed to herself. Somehow, Delta thought, scaring Megan Osbourne at all would be an incredibly difficult thing to do.

13

Staring at the open matchbook and notepad gave Delta a headache. The hieroglyphics scribbled on both was beginning to drive her crazy. More than once, she questioned whether or not to just give it up; whatever "it" was. But she couldn't let go of the image of Miles's face when he told her it was "something big." But did that something get him killed? Was there even a connection? Maybe they had just pulled a job and were afraid of getting caught, or maybe one of them had a warrant out for their arrest.

And maybe not.

Flipping the matchbook over, Delta looked down at Megan's number. Twice, since their meeting the night before, Delta picked up the phone to call her, but she felt like an awkward teenager.

Staring at the phone, as if willing it to ring, Delta shook her head at her prepubescent actions and picked it up. So what if she found the company of a prostitute more pleasurable than her friends right now?

Before the third ring, a woman answered.

"Can I speak with Megan, please?" Delta felt her heart beating loudly.

"Delta! It's good to hear from you." Megan's voice rose and dropped like the violin section of an orchestra. "How are you?"

"Okay, I guess."

"You're having a tough time of it, aren't you?"

Swallowing hard, Delta nodded. At work, it was like she was a ghost; everything she touched felt intangible. Sometimes she was there; sometimes she wasn't.

"I go back to the streets tonight . . . with a new partner. I'm not sure I'm ready for that."

"I'll bet. You sound so hollow."

"I feel hollow, and the thought of a new partner just doesn't work for me right now."

"Give yourself some time. No one said moving on would be easy. It's okay to feel uneasy about it."

Delta wiped her palm on her jeans. It was good talking to someone with a sympathetic ear who did more than talk about what a good cop Miles was.

Heaving a long sigh, Delta switched ears with the phone. "It's just that it's so much harder than I thought. You know, when you get dumped or divorced, you have time to prepare yourself to be with someone new. But this is different. I don't know."

"What can I do for you, Delta?"

"I know you're really busy and everything, and I don't want to get in the—"

"Would you like to meet me for coffee or something after work?"

A hundred-pound weight seemed to lift off Delta's shoulders. "Would you mind?"

"Mind? I'd love to. I had a wonderful time last night."

"Me, too."

The line was silent for a minute.

"Is there something else?"

Delta nodded and switched ears again. "If it isn't too much trouble, I was wondering if you could get a list of everyone in your building."

"Which one? Where I live or where I work?"

"Where you work. But be careful and don't let on what you're doing."

"Gotcha. I'll have it for you first thing in the morning. Why don't you pick me up at the hotel around three-ish?"

Delta felt her smiling through the phone lines. "That'd be great."

"I'm glad I can help. Anything else?"

"You've already done enough."

"Oh, I don't think so, but we can discuss that later. Take care of yourself tonight. I don't want to be stood up because you've gone and got yourself shot or stabbed."

Delta was grinning widely. "I've never stood up a beautiful woman."

"So Miles was right. You do find me attractive. Or does that mean that you only stand up ugly women?"

This brought a chuckle from Delta. It had been so long since she laughed, she almost forgot what it sounded like.

"See you at three. And, thanks."

"Wait till you get my bill." And with another short burst of laughter, Megan hung up.

14

As soon as she pulled into the overcrowded parking lot of the station, she knew something big had gone down.

Parking on the road adjacent to the station, Delta stared out at the mass of people with microphones and cameras. "What in the hell?" she muttered, jumping out of the truck. Before her feet even hit the ground, Connie had her by the arm and was pulling her to the other side of the truck.

"Go through the back," Connie ordered, grabbing Delta's jacket sleeve and pulling her toward the back stairs.

"What's going on?" Delta demanded as they entered the safe confines of the station. "What happened?"

"Hammond was shot and killed early this morning."

"What?" Delta stopped, frozen with memories of that fateful night now echoing in the corridor of the patrol room. "How?"

Connie sucked in a deep breath. "The Captain thinks we may have cop killers on our hands. Thinks the same guy killed Miles."

"Witnesses?"

Connie shook her head. "Not exactly."

Delta felt her legs get weak and sat down. "Where was Larson?"

"Apparently, not in the immediate area. He did see the van, though."

Delta's eyebrows shot up. "You're kidding? Are you sure it was the same van?"

Connie shook her head again. "That's what the press wants to know. That, and how these guys keep getting through the nets."

Delta covered her face with her hands. The hubbub around the station acutely reminded her of the morning's activity after Miles was killed.

"You okay?" Getting Delta a glass of water, Connie rushed back and handed it to her.

Delta took a small sip. Her insides felt on fire. "So . . . the ravenous reporters are into their cop-killer story? God, they're vultures." Drinking the remainder of the water, Delta leaned back in the chair and gazed out the window at the tumultuous gathering in the parking lot, thankful that Connie saved her from any impromptu interviews.

Turning her attention from the crowd, Delta watched a thin, angular man approaching her. It was Frank Taggart, a mediocre cop she had gone to the Academy with. A thick dislike for him had sprouted in the Academy because he was a corner-cutter. If he could do something faster, he would cut any corner to do so.

"Hi, Stevens. Did ya hear the news?"

Delta nodded. He reminded her of a gnat buzzing annoyingly around her ear.

"Looks like we're going to have to watch our backsides out there. Two men down in one week. It's insane."

Delta looked hard at him. "What do mean, 'we?'"

Taggart stepped back from the window. "Didn't you hear? We're partners." Taggart reached a scrawny hand out, which Delta shook with little enthusiasm. This wasn't what she needed to start back to work.

"I know I've got some big shoes to fill, but I'll give it everything I've got. Miles was a great guy and all—"

"I'm sure you will, Taggart. Look, this is my first night back on the street, and I'd appreciate it if we just wouldn't talk about Miles."

"Hey, sure. Fine by me."

Delta rose and her five-nine frame towered over the diminutive Taggart. "Is Captain going to muster when he's through with the press?"

Taggart shook his head. "Severet's got it. He'll fill everyone in. It's a madhouse out there. It makes me wonder if it's really worth putting the badge on every night."

Great, Delta thought grimly. A partner questioning his career was of no use to another cop. They were the greatest hazard on the street because their indecision usually put people's lives on the line. Fill Miles's shoes? Frank Taggart wasn't fit to shine them.

At muster, they learned that Hammond had been shot in the back while checking around the back of a drugstore. His partner, Larson, was maintaining the front of the building. After the shot, he ran around the building, in time to see the van head down the road. License number ZAP 914. The Captain warned there was a possible cop-killing maniac on the loose, and for everyone to be on their toes.

Five minutes after muster, Delta grabbed a radio, jammed it in her holder, and headed for the car, Taggart in tow.

"This guy — this cop-killer. You think maybe he's an ex-con or something?"

Delta shrugged. She was still reading Larson's report. "It was inconceivable to her that the killers were using the same van."

"Who knows?" Delta did not feel like engaging in small talk.

"What are you looking for in that report? You've been studying it like the Bible."

Gritting her teeth, Delta put the report down. "Doesn't it strike you odd that they haven't dumped that van?"

"Maybe they're just stupid."

"Maybe. If they're so stupid, how are they getting through all our nets and perimeters?"

Taggart shrugged. "Who knows. But staring at that report isn't gonna give you the answers. You haven't changed much since the Academy."

Delta picked the report up. "Neither have you, Taggart. Neither have you."

15

Grateful that the shift was over and Taggart could finally stop filling the airwaves with his mindless drivel, Delta walked into the station, motioned for Connie to meet her in the bathroom, and picked up the rest of Larson's report. Before she could make it to the bathroom, Captain Williams barked at her to come into his office.

"Yes, sir."

"How did it go tonight?" he asked, not kindly.

"If you must know, I don't think it will work, sir. We have two different philosophies out there."

"Make it work. You made it work with Brookman, do the same with Taggart."

"He's a long way from being Miles, sir."

"Look, Stevens, I know having a new partner is difficult, but you and Taggart will remain a team until we catch the bastard who's blowing us off the streets."

"Yes, sir."

"And another thing. The media has sunken its teeth into the cop-killings. When they contact you for a statement, you are to have no comment. Do you understand?"

Delta nodded.

"There's enough going on without pulling officers into the limelight."

"Yes, sir. Is that all?"

Captain Williams grinned like the Cheshire cat. "That's all."

Delta nodded and turned to leave, but remembered one more thing. "Captain, who was backup for Hammond and Larson? The report never indicated."

The grin immediately disappeared from his face. "Patterson and McKlinton. Why?"

"Just curious. It wasn't listed in the report, and I was just wondering. Have a nice night, sir." Exiting his office,

Delta headed for the women's room, Larson's complete report tucked under her arm.

"What in the hell are you up to?" Connie asked the moment the door closed.

After checking each stall to be sure they were alone, Delta reached in her shirt pocket and pulled out photocopies of the numbers from the notepad and handed them to Connie.

"What are these?"

Delta shrugged. "I don't know. I was wondering if you and Eddie might be able to decipher them."

Connie looked at the numbers, to Delta, and back at the numbers again. "That depends. What, specifically, are you looking for?"

Delta shrugged. "I wish I knew."

Gazing down at the numbers, Connie nodded. "Well, they all have the same amount of numbers, many begin with the number seven, and there appears to be an abundance of threes and not very many ones."

Delta grinned, admiring the quickness with which Connie's mathematical genius could work.

Folding the paper, Connie stuffed it in her back pocket. "Eddie's going to love this challenge. We've been working on a program that can sort all kinds of numbers, but it's far from perfect. This may take a while."

Delta nodded, touching Connie thankfully on the shoulder. "You're a peach."

"No, a peach would tell you to let go of it. A peach would say it's not important anymore and why risk your own life for something you don't have the faintest idea of. Whatever Miles was investigating should be buried with him."

Delta stood taller, in defiance.

"But I know you, Storm. Those would be empty words. Even after three years on the street, there are still times when you put yourself on auto pilot and cruise right into situations you'd be better off staying away from. I can't say that I blame you, though. Finishing whatever he started might be a source of therapy, and it might give his death a sense of closure in your own life."

"God, Connie, you and Gina have been at it a long time. You sound just like her."

"We've been discussing this. Why else have you grabbed onto it with bulldog determination? In a way, it keeps him alive within you."

"Maybe that's it. Even if I wanted, I couldn't let this go. It drives me day and night."

Connie grinned. "I know. Just don't let it drive you crazy."

Nodding, Delta slowly pulled away. "I won't. Do the best you can with those numbers."

Connie nodded. "Do you have any other leads?"

"Just one. I don't know what it has to do with those numbers, but I'm on my way to get more pieces now."

"Honey, don't burn yourself out on this. Go home, get some rest. You're still healing, you know. Take some time."

Kissing Connie on the cheek, Delta winked, "Tell Eddie I'll buy him a girlfriend or maybe a new modem if he can figure this one out."

"You're going to ignore me, aren't you?"

Delta nodded. "Would you ease off me if I told you that the lead I'm going to talk to tonight is a long-legged, extremely goodlooking blonde?"

Connie's face brightened. "No kidding?"

"No kidding."

"Do I know her?"

"Not yet. But you will." Just thinking about being with Megan brought a smile to her face.

"Well, go get it, girl."

Ten minutes later, Delta pulled up to the motel and found Megan casually leaning against a "no parking" sign. It was only two-thirty.

"You're early," she said, as her long legs folded into the cab of the truck.

"So are you."

"I told him I had a real date and charged him half price." Megan's soft smile filled the cab with warmth. "How was your night?"

"Awful. They gave me this jerk for a partner. The night felt like a week long."

Megan touched Delta's shoulder. "I'm sorry."

"Have you listened to the news?"

Megan shook her head.

"Another cop was gunned down."

Keeping her hand on Delta's shoulder, Megan drew in a deep breath. "It's scary to think that someone would actually go after cops."

"You're telling me."

Pulling into the small, twenty-four hour coffee shop off her beat, Delta opened the door for Megan and admired her shapely rear end as it swished through the front door.

"Why, Officer Stevens, you're worse than a man," Megan teased, not even turning around.

"I'm sorry," Delta fumbled, feeling at once awkward and embarrassed.

"Don't be," Megan flashed that one smile. "I might have been insulted had you not admired my body."

After they ordered, Megan pulled a slip of scented stationery out and slid it over to Delta. "These are the names of everyone who rents out of the hotel."

Delta looked down at the list of twenty or so names, most of them women. "This is excellent. Thank you." Delta looked up from the list to find Megan's gentle smile beaming on her.

"You and Miles are a lot alike," Megan said softly. "You both work too hard and don't know when to stop and smell the roses."

"I'll stop and smell them as soon as I know what's going on."

Megan shook her head and slowly snatched the stationery back. "I'm afraid that just won't do. That won't do at all." Leaning to within a foot of Delta's face, Megan's smile faded. "Your people are getting blown away left and

right. Running around, chasing after Miles's ghost is fine
. . . up to a point."

"And that point is?"

"Until it endangers your well-being. Delta, you look
exhausted. When I touched your shoulder, your muscles
were bunched up like a bag of golf balls. Can we take care
of business and then drop it for tonight?"

Delta nodded. "That would be nice."

Megan smiled. "Great. I didn't want to have to twist your
arm." Putting the list back on the table, Megan pointed to
the two male names at the bottom. "These guys are bad
news. They're into everything from prostitution to hot cars."

"Drugs?"

Megan nodded. "That's how they get their girls."

"Thugs?"

"Not hardly. They rake in some big bucks. These guys
are the business suit variety. They live in the suite."

Delta jotted down notes next to their names. "Did Miles
ever make contact with them?"

"Not that I know of."

"I'll run a check on all of them."

"You won't find many of the girls. A lot of the names on
the sheet are aliases. I don't know most of their real names."

Delta nodded. "Put an asterisk by the women servicing
any cops."

"Are you kidding? Most of them on that list."

Folding the stationery and smelling the lilac perfume,
Delta wondered if Megan hadn't purposely used the scented
stationery.

"One more thing." Delta pulled out the rough sketch of
the tattoo/birthmark she was able to outline for Jonesy four
days after her initial composite. "Have you ever seen this?"

Megan studied it carefully. "No, I haven't."

Delta nodded. The picture had been taken to every
tattoo parlor in the city, and a few said it was the trademark
of a street gang known as the Bandeleros. They were a

motorcycle gang trying to fit into the Hell's Angels mold and not very successful at it.

"Can we finish now?" Megan asked, interrupting Delta's thoughts.

"I'm sorry. Sure."

"Great. Then come on." Grabbing the check, Megan paid the bill and headed outside. A slight mist was falling and the fog partly blocked the three-quarter moon.

"Let's walk," Megan said, threading her arms through Delta's.

"But it's raining."

Megan stopped and jammed her hands on her hips. "Let me get this straight — you face people with guns, knives, and bombs, orgies, weirdos, and nutcases every night of the week, yet you're afraid of a little rain? Officer Stevens, I must say, I'm disappointed."

Delta tossed her head back and laughed. "Alright, I'll go, I'll go."

Walking along in the neon flashes of the dew-covered city, Delta felt the tension ease away.

"Isn't this lovely?" Megan stopped at the edge of a small park. It was dark and the squeaking of the swings swaying in the slight breeze sounded through the air. "It's a beautiful night for a walk."

Delta released Megan's arm from hers and took a step back. There was a rumbling in her stomach, a zip of lightning flashing through her veins, that signaled to Delta just what was going on inside her. Suddenly, there was an emotional overload as her circuits sparked and fired — slowly at first, from disuse, until they finally managed a bright and warming glow inside her. As Delta turned to look at Megan, she was afraid.

"Megan, why are you here, with me?" Before Delta could stop herself, the words tumbled out of her mouth. And though she was surprised by the question, Megan Osbourne was not.

"I need a clarification of the question first. Are you asking why I'm here with you because you're a cop and I'm a prostitute, or are you asking why I'm with you because you're a woman who is attracted to me?"

Delta's only response was a silent, open mouth.

Knowing and seeing the effects of her frankness, Megan's eyes sparkled. "Delta Stevens, I have been enamored with you since the very first day Miles spoke of you. Every single time we met, I always asked what was going on in your life. I knew when you hurt, when you were happy, when the kittens were sick. And when Miles finally showed me that picture of the two of you he kept in his wallet, I knew I had to meet you. Delta, you sounded like someone that I would love to know. Everything he told me about you, I locked away in some hidden file in my mind. If you were as open-minded as Miles said you were, I knew we could be friends. I've been wanting that."

Delta did not know what to say.

"Say something. Please."

Somewhere, somehow, Delta found her voice. "You know I have kittens?"

Megan flashed her a smile. "I know a whole lot more about you than you'd imagine."

Delta nodded. "So you're here with me because you've been wanting to meet the woman Miles spoke of?"

Megan stepped closer — pinning Delta against the park sign. Delta could see Megan's breath as it sensuously floated out and twisted away into the night.

"I'm here with you now, for the same reason you're with me; because I'm alone in this world, because I enjoy your company, because I'd really like to get to know you better, and . . ." Megan paused for emphasis, "Because I am incredibly attracted to you."

16

Walking out of the elevator, Delta approved of the expensive wallpaper with fancy gold trim.

"This is nice," she said, trying not to sound surprised. What did she know about the private lives of prostitutes, anyway? What did she expect? A hovel?

Following Megan to the second door on the right, Delta leaned over and smelled the sweetness of Megan's hair. There was a honey tint that was tangible in its sweetness.

Megan opened the door and turned on the light, displaying a living room decorated in mint and peach. "It's small, but it's home."

Carefully surveying the room, Delta eyed the antique brass lamps and three Nagel prints hanging on one cream-colored wall. The living room was immaculate and smelled new.

"Very nice," she said, slipping her arms out of her jacket.

"Thank you. I may not work in the best joint in town, but I do live in one."

"It's cozy." Sitting next to Megan on an "L" shaped couch, Delta grinned. "It feels like you."

Megan leaned over toward Delta, grinning. "Oh? And what do I feel like?"

Delta drew in a quick breath. Her inner circuitry seemed to fire. "Like an incredible woman. Like someone I want to get to know."

Still leaning in, Megan's blouse blossomed to show an abundant cleavage. "You're awfully sweet."

"It's just that the room reminds me of your eyes. They take you in and make you feel at home."

Megan leaned back and crossed her long legs. "You can believe me when I tell you that they don't do that with everybody."

Delta could feel a blush coming on. Or maybe, it was Megan. Whichever it was, a warmth started from her face and spread down her legs. "I'm not sure I should be here, you know."

Megan's hand reached for Delta's. "Because I'm a prostitute, or because there's someone else?"

Delta stood up quickly and jammed her hands in her pockets. Megan's bluntness tore at the loose thread of her security. "There's no one else. It's just that, lately, I've found myself questioning everything that touches my life."

"And have I done that?"

Delta turned, hands still in her pockets. "Oh, yes."

Joining Delta at the fireplace, Megan slowly reached her hand up to touch Delta's face. "Are you sorry?"

Cocking her head, Delta looked up into Megan's face. She was so close, she could smell the wintergreen of Megan's breath. "No, I'm not sorry. Two weeks ago, I would have allowed my career to keep me from experiencing something wonderful with you, but not any longer. I guess, when someone close to you dies, you begin to realize how little time we have on this planet."

Megan nodded. "I've thought about that myself."

Taking her hands from her pockets, Delta took Megan's and pulled her so close their bodies were touching.

"All I've been doing lately is thinking. I think about that night, I think about Miles's kids, I think about what my life will be like without him, and . . . I think about the feelings banging around in my heart for you. I don't want to think anymore, Megan. I just want to feel."

Wrapping her arms around Delta, Megan held her tightly and stroked her wavy brown locks. For long moments, no words passed between them as Delta's grip slowly tightened around Megan's waist. The heat from their bodies seemed to be the only thing that penetrated the cold stone walls Delta erected the moment Miles died. As they stood entwined, Delta felt her body go limp in Megan's embrace. It felt so good to be held.

At last, it was Megan who spoke. And when she spoke, her voice carried the softness of background music. "That's it. Don't fight your feelings, just go with it."

Saying nothing, Delta buried her face deeper into Megan's neck.

"I know what you need," Megan whispered, kissing Delta's temple. "Will you trust me?"

Delta nodded. Megan's lips against her forehead warmed her more. "I'll try."

"Come with me." Taking Delta's hand, Megan led her into a rose-colored bedroom with a large queen-size waterbed grandly occupying the center. Megan reached out and stroked Delta's cheek with the back of her hand. Her sapphire gems practically glowing in the dim light.

Delta took Megan's hand off her face and kissed the palm. It was softer than she could imagine.

"First things first," Megan said, slowly pulling her hand away from Delta's mouth. "Stay here. I'll be right back." Megan left the room, and Delta looked around at the dusty rose comforter inviting her.

In an instant, Megan returned with a strange-shaped bottle she set on the nightstand. Then she laid her hands on Delta's shoulders. "I'm going to work those golf balls out of your shoulders once and for all. Do you mind?"

Delta shook her head. All she could feel was Megan's soft breath and the stroke of her hands.

Facing Delta, Megan slowly undid the buttons on Delta's shirt and gently slid it off her shoulders. In another smooth motion, Megan undid Delta's bra and removed it as well. Pulling Delta to her, Megan bent down and lightly kissed Delta's neck before facing her.

"Tell me to stop if I make you uncomfortable."

Delta nodded. She felt as if she was going to burst.

Tracing Delta's eyebrows with her finger, Megan stepped closer and Delta again felt her breath on her face. It was an even sweeter aroma than the perfume. A rod of heat from Megan's kiss zipped through her body, landing in the deepest part of her stomach. She had forgotten how it felt to want another woman.

Taking Delta's face in her hands, Megan brought it to hers and softly laid her lips on Delta's. Standing half a foot apart, they tenderly kissed, and Megan slowly moved them closer to the bed.

Closing her eyes and allowing Megan to lead, their lips gently moved over each other's as if they had always known how to kiss each other. Their lips were a perfect fit even as Delta opened her mouth wider to accept Megan's soft tongue. Sliding her hands around Megan's waist, Delta started to pull her closer, but Megan stood firm.

"Not yet," Megan whispered. Patting the bed, Megan motioned for Delta to lie on her stomach. In one swift motion, Megan had Delta's pants off, leaving Delta in just her black underwear.

Laying her face on a pillow that smelled like Megan, Delta's eyes suddenly felt very heavy. The warmth of the waterbed and the fluffy down comforter enveloped her in an instant, and the warmth she felt moments ago transformed into something else. Wrapping her arms around the pillow, Delta drew it to her face and inhaled its sweetness.

"Okay sweety," Megan said, picking up the bottle of lotion. "You just lay there and let me work those knots out of your back. Don't talk, don't think about anything except my hands on your body." Megan's voice was soft and low, almost unrecognizable, and there was a soothing quality that flowed through Delta's veins like a drug, forcing her heavy eyelids to close.

As Megan's fingers slowly pressed and swirled, manipulating Delta's skin and muscles, Delta could feel the tension and coils unwind. In a few minutes, Delta's head sunk deeper into the down pillow. Clouds and stars floated across her consciousness as she drifted between sleep and awareness. Somewhere in the dream landscape of her being, she could hear a low, husky voice speaking calmly and evenly to her as magic feathers brushed across her shoulders and back, warming every inch of skin on her body. Far away, the voice was telling her that she'd be okay, that she wasn't alone, and that she didn't have to fight this battle by herself.

As the last grasp of reality slipped quietly away, Delta felt small, tender kisses on her neck and back and thought she heard Megan say something about later. The next instant, sleep consumed her.

17

The room was veiled in semi-darkness when Delta cracked open one eye and gazed about. Remembering that she was not in her own bed, Delta opened both eyes. Under her left arm Delta found Megan curled up in the crook, breathing evenly and quietly. She was facing Delta and was laying with her knees pulled up to her chest. In her sleep, she was even more breathtaking; her skin was a soft, creamy apricot color, and she could easily pass for nineteen or twenty. As her blonde hair lay scattered about the pillow, Delta leaned over and gently rubbed her face in its silkiness.

Slowly moving her right hand to Megan's face, Delta lightly brushed the hair away from her face and kissed her forehead. Her hair smelled of lilac, and Delta remembered the smell of the pillow in the early morning hours and the softness of Megan's hands as they gently kneaded her back. She vaguely remembered feeling the bed shift and wave when Megan slipped into bed next to her some hours ago. Leaning over, Delta dropped tiny kisses on Megan's cheeks, nose, and chin. As she did, Megan scooted closer and reached up with one slender finger and touched it to her own lips. When she removed her finger, Delta bent over and delicately laid her lips on top of Megan's awaiting mouth. Locked in a tender, morning-warm kiss, Delta pulled Megan to her, feeling her own body temperature escalate as their bodies met. Without taking her lips off Megan's, Delta slipped her hands up and down Megan's back, feeling the soft silk from her rose nightgown.

The warm in Delta turned hot.

Slowly rolling the two of them over so that Megan was on top, Delta hugged her tightly. For a long, silent minute, the two women simply embraced.

Pulling away and flipping her hair over her shoulder, Megan stared down into Delta's face. The strength and meaning of her look was so intense, so powerful, Delta thought she would explode right there.

"I want you, Delta Stevens. Since the day Miles showed me your picture, I've wanted to know you, to be with you."

Skimming her fingertips across Megan's face, Delta smiled. "Then I should be angry with him for never introducing us." Her smile grew. The weight of Megan's body on hers brought such pulsing sensations to her lower body, she wondered if Megan could feel them as well.

"In a way, he did." Kissing Delta's fingers, Megan sucked on the knuckle of Delta's index finger. Eyes closed, tongue moving slowly about the knuckle, Megan started a fire burning in Delta unlike any she had ever felt.

Sensuously pulling Delta's finger from her mouth, Megan lowered her face to Delta's ear and nibbled on her earlobe. "Does the rest of you taste as good?" Megan's voice was so husky and scratchy, it sent tremors down Delta's spine.

"Oh God," Delta heard herself say from far off in some other dimension. Running her hands through Megan's hair while feeling Megan's tongue explore her ear and neck, Delta gently tugged at Megan's negligee until it slipped off her shoulders and dropped silently to the floor.

"You feel so incredible," Delta murmured, running her hands along Megan's smooth shoulders and tight back. When her hands reached the soft arch leading to her butt, Delta could feel a velvet line of peach fuzz running the length of the arch. After stroking the tiny hairs, Delta reached for the two fleshy cheeks slowly moving into her. They were the softest things she had ever felt.

As the waterbed moved in sync with their connected rhythm, Delta braced herself as Megan slid her tongue slowly down her neck, slowly across her chest, and ever so slowly around her breast. Around and around Megan sensuously moved her skilled tongue until finally, when Delta could no longer stand the torment, it slipped up and over her nipple, sending jolts of heat and electricity through Delta's entire being.

"You're driving me crazy," Delta moaned, clutching Megan's head to her chest.

"That's the idea," Megan whispered between nibbles. "Want me to stop?"

"No. God, no."

Megan looked up and smiled into Delta's face. "I didn't think so."

Sliding her body between Delta's legs, Megan inched her way down Delta's flat stomach, sometimes biting, sometimes kissing the taut skin leading to the dark patch of hair inviting her. Laying her cheek against Delta's stomach, Megan gingerly stroked Delta's inner thighs, occasionally brushing against the curly mound. Each time she did this, a soft moan escaped Delta's parted lips.

"You have one of the most incredible bodies I have ever seen," Megan whispered, feeling the strong muscles in Delta's thighs and running her slender fingers over the chiseled stomach.

Delta couldn't respond. Her legs were on fire, her stomach singed from where Megan had laid her face, and every inch of her wetness scorched from the desire burning beneath the surface.

Slowly moving her face back toward Delta's, Megan lingered around Delta's breasts, allowing her hair to brush lightly across the already hard nipples.

Arching her back, Delta released Megan's head and gripped the comforter in both hands. It was a non-verbal plea.

Looking down into Delta's face, Megan gently lowered her moist lips onto Delta's and slid her tongue quietly into Delta's eagerly awaiting mouth. As they kissed like lovers who had known each other forever, their bodies locked like two pieces of a jigsaw. Over and over, Megan's tongue darted in and out of Delta's mouth, enticing her, teasing her, sending her to places Delta had only dreamt about. As her tongue plunged once more between Delta's lips, Megan slowly moved her hand between Delta's legs and caressed the brown hair.

As she accepted Megan's soft tongue, Delta's whole body shuddered as Megan's slender fingers explored her burning wetness. Stroke after stroke, Delta waited for Megan's gentle fingers to glide across the special place aching to be touched.

As the two women melded together, moving in unison, communicating in the universal language, Delta's body felt as if it burst into flames. In one beautiful and engaging moment, Delta's entire being flooded with firey liquid that blasted through her veins like an erupting volcano. Like heat from an inferno, Delta's body and spirit glowed.

She wanted to say something, wanted to tell Megan how wonderful it was, but she couldn't find the words. Instead, she rolled over on top of Megan and buried her face in her long, slender neck. For what felt like hours, she nuzzled Megan's neck and shoulders while her hands cupped the perfectly round breasts and tenderly squeezed them.

Raising her head from Megan's lilaced shoulders, Delta looked down into the beautiful face beaming up at her.

"I don't know what to say," Delta whispered, staring down into the eyes that were bluer than she had remembered.

Caressing Delta's cheek with the back of her hand, Megan gently kissed her. "Then don't say anything. Show me."

Returning Megan's kiss with renewed passion, Delta did just that.

18

Sitting across from Megan at the small brass and glass table, Delta reached across and held Megan's hand. The silence between them was filled with warm words and emotions. For long pauses, they looked at each other over two steaming cups of coffee. As the steam swirled and rose, entangling as each line met halfway, two slow grins crept across their faces. The room illuminated under their knowing smiles. It was as if all that needed to be said had already been shared. For Delta, it was a peacefulness that slowly moved in and around her battered heart, making reparations and healing the wounds. It was the much needed tenderness her broken spirit needed.

"Thank you," Delta said above the steam from the coffee.

"For what? Doing something I've laid in bed dreaming about?"

Delta shook her head. "That's not what I meant. I mean thank you for being here — for caring."

Megan reached across the table and held Delta's hand. "You're even more special than Miles said you were. Caring about you is easy."

Delta grinned. "I'm so glad. This morning was incredible."

Megan donned a grin that matched Delta's. "It was, wasn't it?" Bringing Delta's hand to her lips, Megan lightly brushed her lips across her palm.

Suddenly, the grin faded from Delta's face, replaced by knitted brows. "Megan—"

Before Delta could finish, Megan placed a finger over Delta's lips. "No, Delta, that isn't how it is when I work. You had all of me; my mind, my emotions, my spiritual energy — all of it was in your grasp."

Delta looked away. "I'm sorry. I didn't want to say anything."

Megan left her chair and kneeled down in front of Delta, taking both hands in hers. "I understand. But I need you to understand as well. You and I made love, Delta. We shared a part of each other's souls. When you kiss me or touch me, there's a delight, a passion for you that consumes me. Work isn't like that. I don't feel anything. It's all an act. But with you, all I did was feel. I felt your desire, your hunger, your—"

"Love?"

A gentle smile curved on Megan's face. "Yes."

Delta said nothing. Looking down into Megan's crystal eyes, Delta knew she had felt it, too.

As Megan rose, she stepped on the files Delta had brought in from the truck. Picking up one of the reports, Megan studied it carefully before setting it down and shaking her head.

"All those codes would be enough to drive me crazy. Wouldn't it be easier to call it a murder instead of a — what is it? A 187? That's so impersonal."

Delta sipped her coffee and nodded.

"And it never ceases to amaze me how you cops can see these tiny license plate numbers from so far away. I mean, do you have bionic vision or what?"

Delta's eyebrows suddenly lifted. "What did you say?"

"I said, I don't see how you can tell these letters from so far away."

Delta grabbed the report and looked over it. Quickly spotting one of the incongruencies, Delta lowered the report and smiled at Megan. "That's it."

"What?"

"There were some things about his report that have been gnawing at me, but I wasn't able to get a grip on it."

"What's that?"

"It's really been bugging me that the killers didn't dump that van."

Megan nodded, "I'll say. They're just asking to get caught."

Delta stared down at the report. "It looks that way, doesn't it?"

"So what's your point?"

Delta handed Megan the report. "Look at the report. What time does it say Hammond and Larson responded to the drugstore call?"

Megan read from the report. "Approximately Oh-four-eleven. See what I mean? You don't even tell time like regular people."

Delta grinned at her perception before returning her gaze to the report. "Okay. So they respond at Oh-four-eleven. When does it say Hammond was shot?"

"According to Officer Larson, he was shot at Oh-four-sixteen."

"Five minutes later."

Megan nodded, her eyes lighting up.

"When did Larson call for help?" Delta kneeled in front of Megan with her hands on Megan's knees.

"Oh-four-sixteen and ten seconds."

"Ten seconds after he heard the shot?"

Megan nodded. "I guess so."

Delta grabbed the reports and jammed them all back in the envelope. "Are you busy after class?"

Megan smiled. "Well ... gee ... are you asking me out?"

Delta grinned back at her. "Not exactly. I need your help."

Megan leaned over and kissed Delta. "I thought you'd never ask."

* * * * * * * *

Pulling up to the drugstore where Hammond was killed, Delta and Megan exchanged curious glances. It was a small, one-story square building attached on either side to two other larger buildings. It was not, as Delta believed, a solitary, single-standing building. Instead it was the second from the corner, looking nearly abandoned with its barred windows and padlocked front door. Delta estimated the total footage in front of the three buildings to be at least eighty yards, maybe more. Add to that another eight-plus yards of the side of the building for a total distance of over one hundred and fifty yards.

"The report says that Hammond dropped Larson off in the back of this building before making his way to the front by car." Megan looked out at the building. "He must have really burned some rubber if he made it around this building in ten seconds."

Delta nodded. "My thoughts exactly."

"You don't think he made it, do you?"

"Drop me off in the back and let's find out. When you get to the front, honk the horn and time how long it takes me to get there."

Megan eyed the building. "More than ten seconds, even if you are in good shape." Reaching over, Megan stroked Delta's inner thigh. "And believe me, you're in great shape."

Hopping out of the truck, Delta walked to the back of the store.

As soon as she rounded the corner, she heard the blast of her truck's horn and took off running in a dead sprint. It felt as if she was running forever by the time she reached the corner and turned toward the front of the building.

"Hhhow long?" she asked, winded by her all-out run.

"Twenty-five."

"And that's in tennis shoes." Leaning into the truck, Delta set the trip timer to zero. "Let's try the same thing. Only this time, after honking the horn, wait five seconds and take off down the street. Keep going until the clock hits twenty, then stop. Wait a few seconds before coming back."

Megan nodded; her face veiled in seriousness.

"Enjoying yourself?" Delta asked, resisting the urge to kiss her full lips.

Megan winked at her. "Having the time of my life."

"You're a cheap date," Delta cracked, taking off down the alley.

"Only for you, honey."

When the horn honked again, Delta started off quickly. When she rounded the corner, her truck was nowhere in sight.

A few seconds later, Megan pulled into the parking lot.

"He never could have seen the van," Megan announced, moving over for Delta to get in.

"He said he not only saw the van, but read the same plate."

"Not possible."

"It doesn't appear so."

"I was well out of sight even in the ten-second range. You didn't stand a chance to tell which direction I headed, let alone read my license plate. Which, by the way, if I had killed a cop, I wouldn't have."

"Then Larson's lying."

Megan stared at Delta. "But why?"

"I wish I knew."

"You think this has something to do with Miles?"

"I'm beginning to think there's a connection. I mean, his partner had just been blown away. Did he imagine he saw the van, or is he purposely trying to throw the investigation astray?"

"If he imagined the van, Delta, then he also imagined seeing the license plate as well."

Rubbing her chin, Delta stared down at the report. "I'd bet a year's paycheck that the van is under the river somewhere and that Larson never saw the plates or the van."

"So what now?"

Opening the door for Megan, Delta felt a ball of fear well up in her stomach. "Now we try to figure out what Larson is trying to cover up."

As Delta jumped in the cab, a light rain started falling.

"Must we do so this afternoon?"

Delta turned to find Megan's eyes sparkling. "What did you have in mind?"

Scooting closer to Delta, Megan purred in her ear. "I understand you're a pretty decent chess player."

A slow smile spread across Delta's face. "I'm okay."

Megan purred a sensuous laugh. "Okay? Miles said you're very good."

Shifting the truck into first and trying to keep on her side of the road, Delta fumbled for both the words and the gears. "That's because he taught me how to move my pieces better."

Threading her arms around Delta's neck and running her tongue around the inside of Delta's ear, Megan whispered, "And I do love the way your pieces move."

19

"Have you got anything for me yet?" Delta whispered into Connie's ear as she sat glaring into the monitor.

Connie looked around before answering. "Maybe. Eddie thinks they may be a combination of numbers. Just what that combination is, we don't know yet. I say give him a few more working hours, and we might be able to come up with it. What have you got on your end?"

"Not here." Delta left Connie and made her way to the bathroom.

As Connie followed, closing the door, she lowered her voice. "What are you up to?"

Delta replayed for Connie her findings from the afternoon's investigation.

"Storm, What in the hell is going on?"

"I don't know. I'm telling you, Con, Larson never saw that van."

Connie stared down at the computer paper in her hand. "How do these numbers tie in to this?"

Delta shrugged. "We know that Miles was keeping track of cop activity at the Red Carpet. How Hammond's death and Larson's lie fit with the rest of this, I haven't a clue. I'm hoping those numbers tell us something we don't already know."

"So . . . where do we go from here?"

"You and Eddie keep at those numbers. I'm going to go through some recent files and see what sort of activities Larson and Hammond were bringing down."

Connie looked hard at Delta. "If Larson is lying about the van—"

"Then God knows what else he's covering up."

"Cops who cover up are dangerous, Delta. You watch where you stick your nose before you go storming your way into an informal investigation."

Delta nodded. If Larson was purposely trying to throw the investigation into Miles's death askew, she would have a whole lot more to worry about than just her nose.

20

The questions pounded relentlessly at her, and Delta could not push them aside any longer. Why had Larson lied? Delta did not believe he saw the van. She did not believe the same vehicle with the same plates had been used in the second murder. So, were the killers in a different vehicle and Larson knew it? Did he purposely wait to call for backup and that's why they escaped the net? Did he know who the killers were? The questions came to her so much faster than the answers. So Delta decided if the answers wouldn't come to her, she would go to them.

Rifling through the files, trying to be inconspicuous, Delta pulled eight of Larson and Hammond's reports and four of hers and Miles's. Skimming over the reports, she realized that most of Hammond and Larson's activities centered around traffic citations and auto theft. In the past month, no hard collar crimes, and no drug busts of any kind.

"That's odd," Delta mumbled to herself. How could they have no drug-related busts when the activity surrounding their beat had increased dramatically? They had just as much drug activity as she and Miles did, yet they made no busts? It made no sense.

Opening her and Miles's files, Delta counted a number of drug-related busts and one big collar in the past month. Delta grinned, remembering the major bust they made only a few weeks ago. She and Miles got a hot tip on a crack house that was getting ready to close in their area. With a little information and a lot of luck, they were able to collar the owner and five of his main dealers. It had been so exciting. Just looking at all the crack that would never make the streets was their own personal high. A little over 140 pounds was wrapped up for the evidence room, and away from the grasp of children and teens. It was busts like these that reminded her why being a cop was so rewarding.

Shaking the memory away, Delta flipped the report over. Stapled on the reverse side was the evidence tag. At once, Delta stared, dumbfounded at the tag. "What in the —?" Bringing it closer to her face, Delta studied it carefully. Instead of reading 160 pounds, it merely read sixteen.

"Sixteen?" she cried, not caring who heard her. "That's impossible." Slamming the report shut and cramming all the files back into the cabinet, Delta headed downstairs to the evidence room.

"I'm sorry, Stevens, you know the rules. Unless the Captain has signed his okay, you ain't going in."

Delta glared at the officer standing behind the cage. He had his job to do. She understood that much, but she needed to know.

"Look, Trask, I've found an error on my report that may or may not be a typo. I can't take the case to court unless I know for sure; chain of evidence and all. You know."

Trask grunted and rolled his eyes. "What's the number?"

"13496. I need to know if the weight is correct. See if it's sixteen or sixty-one." Delta did not wish to tip her hand completely.

In a minute, Trask came waddling back, grunted, and punched Delta's name in on the computer. "Tag says sixteen. There's sixteen pounds of crack back there. No mistake."

Delta felt the blood rush from her face. This wasn't possible. Leaning on the counter, Delta asked weakly, "Are you absolutely sure?"

"Sixteen, Stevens. One-six. Check for yourself."

Delta carefully watched the monochrome screen as it accepted her name and badge number.

That was odd. She didn't remember getting a memo about signing in.

"Do you sign people in who just make inquiries?"

Trask nodded.

"Have we always done that? I don't remember that always being the procedure."

"Nope. Captain Williams started it a little over a month ago. Any more questions?"

Delta stared at him. Trask was very wrinkled and perennially grumpy — one reason why he was assigned the dungeon. "Did we receive a memo on this?"

Sighing loudly, Trask shrugged. "I don't s'pose the Captain feels the need to explain his actions, do you?"

Delta ignored his sarcasm. "Where does the printout of that list go?"

"To the Captain. The night clerk prints it up and sends one copy to the Captain and one to records."

"Thanks." Taking her evidence tag, Delta ran back upstairs.

"I've got something else I need Eddie for," Delta whispered to Connie.

"Name it."

"I need to know whose names are on the evidence room list."

Connie did not look up from her typing. "What list?"

"Haven't been to the evidence room lately, have you? Captain Williams ordered that everyone's name requesting info be listed on the computer. Is there any way—"

A twinkle lit up in Connie's eye. "Now that's right up our alley. We can tap into that line in nothing flat. It's all in-house, and even if it's locked, Eddie and I can bust in. That's our specialty. But that'll put these other numbers on the back burner for a bit."

"Do it. I have a gut feeling I know whose names are going to show on that list."

"What do you have going, Del?" Connie's eyebrows raised in suspicion.

Looking around to be sure no one was within earshot, Delta's voice dropped to barely a whisper. "One hundred and forty-four pounds of crack are missing from the bust Miles and I had a few weeks ago."

Connie stopped typing and looked hard at Delta. "You mean—"

"That someone has taken that dope out of there and replaced our evidence tag with a phony one."

Connie's eyes widened. "More phony reports?"

"It appears that way."

For a moment, the two women looked at each other as their own fears embedded themselves deep within them.

"Oh Storm, do you realize what this means?"

Delta nodded. "That we've probably discovered what Miles was after."

Connie winced. "So his hornets' nest has now become ours?"

Delta nodded. "If I have anything to say about it, yes."

Turning to leave, Delta reached out and squeezed Connie's neck. "I'm afraid, my friend, that this could get ugly. I'll understand if you want to back out."

Connie did not move her eyes from the screen. "Hey, did Tonto ever skip out on the Lone Ranger? Did Robin ever leave Batman? Did Abbot ever—"

"Thanks, Con. I knew you'd hang in here with me."

Turning from the monitor, Connie's eyes narrowed. "*Hang* is the operative word. It was Ben Franklin who said *We must all hang together, or, most assuredly, we will hang separately.*"

Nodding slowly, grateful to have Connie watching her backside, Delta started for the door. As she threw open the door and gazed out over the darkening city, something inside her turned cold and hard, as brash reality struck her with full force. Deep inside, she knew what was happening, and it left her feeling frozen and ugly.

In her gut, Delta's inner voice told her it was entirely possible that Miles was killed by another cop.

21

The shift had been long and miserable, with Taggart asking too many questions and making her a participant in his small talk. When they finally pulled into the station, Delta headed straight for her car. All night long, she was overwhelmed by the idea that she was now involved in investigating a cover-up.

Walking over to her car, Delta found a note tucked in her wipers. Opening the note, she immediately saw it was Connie's handwriting.

Interesting stuff . . . Eddie, the brat, figured it out. Meet me.

Delta grinned. Connie was good. Looking at her watch, Delta saw that it was only 1:05. She and Taggart knocked off early because he had a court appearance in the morning. This was just another fine example of his corner-cutting.

"Good job," Delta mumbled, slipping the note in her left chest pocket where she carried Miles's badge. Although the note might appear innocuous to anyone snooping around, it told Delta where to meet her and what it was about. Eddie must have figured the code out, and Connie wanted to meet her at The Brat, the bar across from the Red Carpet.

Genius.

Throwing a sweatshirt over her uniform, Delta changed into the high tops she carried in the back.

"A fashion risk at best," Delta said to herself, looking at the dark blue pants with the black stripe that met her black sweatshirt on one end and white Nikes on the other. "Good thing I'm not looking for a date." Reaching into her glove compartment, Delta took out her 9 millimeter and slid it into her ankle holster.

Walking through the parking lot, Delta stopped a moment and let the fine mist of rain fall gently to her face. It was a warmer night than usual, and the rain felt wonderful as it caressed her lashes and cheeks. Delta smiled, remembering Megan chastising her for chasing after hoodlums but not wanting to walk in the rain.

Her smile lingered as thoughts of Megan pushed out all others. Megan. She made Delta feel again. She felt that youthful warmth that seeped in whenever new love sprouted, and she welcomed it with open arms. The emptiness left by Sandy and Miles was slowly closing its yawning gap as Megan's love and compassion bridged the wound. Like the rain, it seemed to refresh her life.

As the mist tickled her cheeks, Delta sighed. The rain, she didn't mind. It was the cold she didn't like, and it had been a colder winter than she could ever remember. There were nights when even her thick leather jacket couldn't . . .

Quickly turning her face from the clouds, Delta's mind churned. It had been very cold the night Miles was killed. She remembered him turning the heat up as soon as they got in the car. That's what hit her; the killer had worn a black tank top — a skimpy black tank top.

Very odd. With such an obvious tattoo, not to mention the freezing weather, he would have worn something over it.

"Unless . . ." Delta said aloud. "Unless he wanted me to see the tattoo."

Delta turned back to the truck and jotted the note down on her pad. Maybe that's why he didn't kill her. Maybe the tattoo was a diversion like Larson's report, it was a false focus for the police.

"How could I be so stupid?" Delta demanded of herself, slamming her pad shut. She was to attest to a tattoo that belonged to some no-named gang in the city that was supposed to be responsible for killing two cops.

Someone carefully orchestrated her every move as the only live witness to a cop's murder.

Shaking her head, Delta entered the bar.

"Hi, Gina," Delta said, bending down to kiss the top of her head.

"Hello, Delta. I see that the two of you are a bit deeper into this than you imagined you would be."

Delta nodded. "And I'm afraid we're only going to go deeper."

Connie motioned the waitress over and ordered Delta a Diet Coke. "You have more, don't you?"

Delta nodded. "I've been struggling with the question about why, if this guy is supposed to be a cop killer, why he didn't kill me, too. Tonight, as I shot out of the truck, I remembered something."

Connie leaned forward. "What?"

"The killer was wearing a tank top, Con. A damned tank top in twenty-degree weather." Delta hesitated for emphasis. "He wanted me to see the tattoo. Someone wants me to believe that Miles was killed by a gang."

Gina and Connie exchanged glances. "That would explain why they didn't shoot the only witness."

"Exactly. The tattoo is a sham meant to lead the investigation astray."

"How does this connect with Larson's phony report?"

Delta rubbed her tired eyes before answering. "His report supports the theory of a cop killer on the loose. Instead of us looking within, as Miles must have been doing, now all our efforts are concentrated on the outside. It's the perfect diversion." Sipping her Diet Coke, Delta leaned over to Connie. "What did you and Eddie find out?"

Letting go of Gina's hand, Connie pushed a computer printout over to Delta. "Eddie was able to get the list from the evidence room. You're not going to like it."

Delta looked at it. For a moment, she did not know what to say. Miles's name appeared over a dozen times on different dates in the past month. "This can't be."

"That's what I thought. According to this, Miles makes it a habit to visit the evidence room."

Delta's eyes scanned the list and the dates. "Miles hated it down there and felt that his job was to arrest people, not push the paperwork around. This doesn't make any sense."

"Tell that to the computer."

"Wait," Delta said as her eyes zeroed in on a date that rang an alarm in her head. "This can't be right."

"What?"

"This says that Miles went to the evidence room not once, but twice on the third. The fact is, Miles was out of town that day."

"Are you sure?"

"Yeah, I am. Remember? His grandmother was getting married, and he and Jennifer went out of town for the weekend."

Connie looked at Gina, who shrugged. "Are you positive?"

"Absolutely. I went out with a training patrol rookie instead. Checking my activity that night will prove that we weren't working together. And a call into Jennifer will confirm that Miles was with her."

"Del, do you realize what you're saying?"

The ball of fear in her stomach grew. "I'm afraid so. Someone has one hundred and forty-four pounds of crack that Miles and I collected from that bust. That someone is one of us." A cold chill ran down Delta's back as her words slid out her mouth. "Miles must have discovered the missing dope as well and—"

"And was that close to finding out who it was."

"So . . ." Delta said, inhaling a painful breath, "they killed him."

For a long, tense moment, the three women sat, quiet in their own anxious thoughts, feeling their own personal fears and trepidation as the data loomed heavily before them. It was incomprehensible that they were after fellow cops; incomprehensible that Miles may have been killed by a colleague.

Connie was the first to move, and slowly put her hands out for both Gina and Delta. As they all held hands, joined by a growing fear and painful silence, Connie slowly, quietly asked, "You've been to the evidence room, haven't you?"

Delta nodded.

"That means they'll know you're on to them."

Delta nodded again.

"If they suspect that you know . . ."

"Then they'll come after me like they did Miles."

Again, the three women lapsed into silence. Somehow, Miles had stumbled onto a pilfering scam at the station. Dirty cops were dirtying the streets with the dope she and Miles had risked their lives to get off the streets. Miles fell into this mess, possibly by accident, and must have seen cleaning it up as his ticket to Vice.

Squeezing hard Gina's hand, Delta fought back the angry tears forcing their way to her eyes. In this one blink of Time's eye, everything she believed in, everything she held dear, was flushed down the toilet and into the stinking sewer below.

"Miles," Delta said slowly, "must have been killed by one of us."

Again, an eerie silence surrounded them. As hard as it was to believe, everything they uncovered pointed in that direction.

"So why was Hammond killed? Think he was working with Miles?"

"Maybe they needed another death to substantiate the cop-killer story." Connie brought Delta's hand to her face and rubbed it against her cheek.

"Maybe."

Gina reached over and held Delta's other hand. "What are we going to do? If they believe you're onto them, your life is in danger."

Connie agreed. "Right now, their story is foolproof. The media have everyone believing that a cop killer is on the loose. If they take you out, you'll just fit right into their story line."

Inhaling deeply, Delta shook her head. "The problem is we have an invalid players' card. We can't trust anyone and that places us at a distinct disadvantage. We can't make a move until we know who all the players are."

"And how do we do that?"

Leaning back, Delta stared into her empty glass. She now knew what Miles must have gone through the weeks before his death. Nothing felt tangible — it was as if they were chess pieces in a chess match being moved by some mysterious power.

"We don't. From here on out, we're on our own."

Connie took the printout and looked at it. She studied it a long time before speaking. "Miles is their out, isn't he? He's their escape valve."

Delta nodded. "Someone has set him up to take the fall should anyone get suspicious. How easy it will be for them to blame it on a dead man. They have all the proof they need right there in that phony list. It's the perfect plan." Delta's eyes burned with anger. "Perfect, but for one major flaw."

Connie nodded. "Us."

"And we are going to flush the bastards out."

Connie looked up from the printout, pupils small as a pinhead. "If I had to bet who typed Miles's name in here, I'd bet it was the person responsible for setting up this sign-in sheet in the first place."

Delta looked at Connie and nodded. It was the only answer.

"Captain Williams."

22

Delta was glad that her weekend had already begun. This way, she had three more days to figure out where to go from here. Rocked by the revelation that her partner had been killed by her brothers in blue, Delta wrestled with the anger and bitterness growing inside. She was angry with herself for not making him talk to her about it. She was mad at Miles for not sharing this with her. Together, they might have been able to work it out. Once he knew what was going down, and they knew he knew, he had very little time with which to work. As it was, his time had run out. He would never make it to Vice.

Laying down on the bed, Delta looked at her uniform hanging on the knob of the door. Being a cop had meant so much to her. She remembered how proud her mother was the day she graduated from the Academy. Delta's three sisters snapped photos like crazy while her mother and Sandy sat proudly in the grandstands. It was the first time she felt as if she really belonged someplace. Now, her badge was tainted with good blood and bad dope. So much of what she believed in was being sold on the corner of the street, and Delta didn't know where to begin to fix it.

Slowly, she got off the bed and pulled her badge off her shirt. Then, she pulled Miles's badge out of her pocket and stared at them a long time. Badge numbers were important to cops because they identified them as someone different from the others. She and Miles used to play games all the time, using their badge numbers as answers. Miles used to say that her badge number, which was 182 read "one lesbian ate two and that made for women stew."

"We were so weird," Delta said aloud, still gazing down at the badges now laying on the bed. For a second, she stared hard at the two badges, before rolling over on her side and quickly dialing the telephone.

"Connie?"

"What's up?" came Connie's voice.

"Try putting my badge number and Miles's badge number into Eddie and see what you come up with."

"182 and 342?"

Delta grinned. "How do you do that?"

"I never forget a number once I see it, you know that."

"Yes, I do, and if I recall correctly, that made you very unpopular in Reno."

Connie's laughter rang through the phone lines. "Hell, they kicked us out because they didn't want a minority to take any money home. So, what am I looking for?"

Delta shrugged. "Miles used to have a thing about badge numbers. He played games with them all the time. Just put those into Eddie along with the list of numbers and see what he comes up with."

"And in the meantime?"

"In the meantime, I need a break from all of this. I think I'll go on a date."

"A date? Is it that gorgeous blonde, Megan?"

Delta smiled. "Yeah."

Connie squealed. "Good for you. It's about time."

Delta nodded. "It sure is."

"Sounds like you're hooked already."

"Maybe. If I wasn't thinking about this case all the time, I'd be thinking about her."

"Good for you. Does she feel the same?"

"I think so. We haven't discussed it much."

There was a short pause on the line before Delta heard Connie draw in a breath. "Delta? There's something else, isn't there?"

Delta only nodded.

"Is she married?"

"No, it's nothing like that."

"Then what?"

Closing her eyes, Delta let it out. "She's a prostitute."

The silence on the end of the line was deafening, and then, in one big roar, she could hear Connie laughing. "Is that all? So what?"

"I thought—"

"You should know me better than that. If she makes you happy, I couldn't give a shit if she ran a block long brothel."

Delta released a huge sigh. "Thanks."

"Don't thank me, thank my parents. They left the Catholic church before I was born. God knows how many pounds of guilt I'd be wearing if they didn't. I'll get back to you as soon as Eddie burps it out."

"Burps it out? Isn't he feeling well?"

"He's got indigestion from this whole thing."

"You be careful. Don't get caught sneaking around inside someone else's software."

This made Connie snickered. "Gina tells me to stay out of other women's underwear, you tell me to stay out of other people's software . . . I'll never have any fun."

"Thanks, Connie. You're a doll." Depressing the receiver, Delta called Megan at home but got no answer. Checking her watch, Delta saw that it was close to seven o'clock. Megan would just be starting work.

Staring out the window, Delta felt a void. This time, it wasn't the void from missing Miles; it was a hole from missing Megan.

Tossing her jacket on, Delta headed out the door. Perhaps if Megan had been missing her too, she could persuade her to take the night off as well.

Hell, it was worth a try.

23

As the fine mist continued winding its way down to the dampened streets, Delta parked her truck a few blocks down the street from the Red Carpet. Opening the door to the mist and cool air, Delta inhaled deeply. She had always loved winter. She and Miles would always share what they were getting everyone for Christmas. He would beam about the toys he bought the kids; toys he usually played with more than they did. He had always shown her the jewelry or sweaters that he bought Jennifer to make sure they weren't ugly. She would miss that more than she had ever imagined.

As Delta turned onto the walkway leading to the hotel, a large man suddenly burst through the doors, rammed into her like a linebacker, and sent her sprawling onto the wet grass. Rolling to her stomach, Delta pulled her 9 millimeter from her ankle holster and drew down on the guy, but he was already hopping into a white Ford pickup with no license plates.

Watching the truck roar out of sight, Delta jumped to her feet and plastered herself against the side of the hotel. Her heart pounded wildly as she regripped her automatic.

As she inched her way to the lobby, Delta could hear the commotion inside. Someone was yelling at someone else to call an ambulance, and another woman was crying loudly. Holding her breath, Delta slammed open the front door, pointing her automatic at the group huddled around the reception desk.

"Police! Don't move! Get your hands where I can see them!" Delta demanded as the group of three women and one male turned to her. Delta quickly took an inventory of the layout of the hotel. There was one hallway, a door for the stairs, and an elevator. From where she stood, she could cut someone down coming through the hallway without taking any heat herself. For the time being, crouched in front of the door, Delta was safe.

"What's going down?" She asked, eyeballing the tiny huddle.

The four people exchanged glances. Delta understood that the code of the streets took precedent over her demands, so she lowered her weapon slightly.

"A friend of mine works here. I came to help."

Before anyone could reply, a woman burst out of a room and ran down the hall. "Where is that fucking ambulance?" She cried.

Suddenly, the hackles on Delta's neck stood up. "Will someone tell me what the hell is going on?"

The woman who came running into the room pointed down the hall. "Some bastard just beat up one of the girls. She's hurt real bad."

"Are there any more men in here?"

The group shook their collective heads. "They all took outta here as soon as they heard the screams."

Still gripping her weapon, Delta turned to the reception desk. "Call the cops. Tell them that there is an off-duty officer on the scene already." As Delta lowered the gun, she motioned with her head for the woman to take her to the room.

"She's usually more careful than that," the woman explained.

"Who?" Delta felt the cold tingles run up and down her arms.

"Her name's Megan."

Suddenly, Delta wheeled around, slipped her gun in the front of her pants, and ran for the reception desk. Without asking any questions, she dove over the counter and slammed her hand down on the phone. "Don't call the cops. Just get an ambulance here, fast. Whatever you do, do not contact the police."

The man at the desk grinned. "I never had any intention of it."

"Good." Whirling around, Delta started down the hall.

"She's in room 102," the woman said, pointing down the darkened hallway.

"Is there anyone in there with her?"

The woman nodded. "Hey man, we know how to take care of each other."

Delta's eyes narrowed. "I can see that."

Pulling her automatic from her waist band, Delta slowly turned the knob to the room.

"Hey, you don't need that thing," the woman whispered, nodding her head to the gun.

Delta ignored her and quickly pushed the door open.

"I'm a cop," Delta said not harshly, pointing the gun into the room. A young black woman of about eighteen stood over the crumpled heap on the bed, holding a compress to the battered face.

For a moment, no one moved. The two women in the room standing next to the bed turned to face Delta, but the third one, who was holding the towel, continued wiping the face with a blood-splattered towel.

"We ain't done nothin'," a heavyset woman said, moving slightly away from the bed.

Delta nodded. "Relax. I'm not here to bust anyone. I came to help." Approaching the bed, Delta's stomach leapt into her throat. She recognized the slender hands with their tapered fingernails. In the flash of an instant that it took her mind to register that the woman on the bed was indeed, Megan, Delta placed her gun into her waistband and dropped to her knees.

"She'll be okay," the black woman offered, handing a towel to Delta. "You Officer Stevens?"

"Yes." Taking the blood-soaked towel from her, Delta smiled gratefully.

"She hollered through the door for me to get you. How you know she needed you?"

"Instinct." Turning back to the heap on the bed, Delta tried to calm her nerves. She had seen mutilated babies, raped women, and battered spouses, but none of it prepared her to see the ravaged face and body of someone she loved.

"Oh God," Delta murmured, looking down at the swollen and bloodied face of Megan. Had it not been for her beautiful hair, Delta wasn't sure she would be able to recognize the woman laying on the bed.

Delta gently applied the cloth to Megan's face and made sure she was still breathing.

"The ambulance is on its way," someone said from behind them.

Megan's face was puffy and blue around the eyes, and her mouth continued bleeding from a large gash in her lower lip. A bump on her forehead appeared to grow right before Delta's eyes, and a gash on her left cheek ran a jagged edge from her temple to her chin. Instantly, Delta knew Megan had taken several hard blows from a man wearing a large ring. Looking at her arms, Delta took notice of several small cuts, most likely from the same ring that hit Megan's face.

Whoever had done this would pay. Whoever had poured the poison into Miles's life and taken him away from her would face justice. It was war now, and Delta promised not to stop until they were all brought down hard. They, whoever they were, would pay — if not with their blood, then with their freedom.

Brushing Megan's hair away from her bloodied face, Delta heard the sirens in the background.

"Megan? Megan, honey, it's me, Delta. Can you hear me?"

Delta felt slight pressure from Megan's hand.

"The ambulance is on its way. You're going to be okay. Can you understand me?" Again, the hand pressed into Delta's, only stronger.

"You've got to be okay. I need you." Turning to the black woman, Delta asked, "Does anyone have any idea of what happened?"

The woman shook her head. "We heard Megan screaming, came running, and scared him off."

"Was it a trick?"

The woman shrugged. "I don't think so. Megan's real good about picking guys. She don't usually hop with a kink."

Nodding, Delta returned her attention back to Megan.

Hearing the sirens get louder, she leaned over and lightly kissed Megan's forehead. Inside her soul, Delta felt her anger dance with the gentle love she was feeling for Megan. The wiring in her spirit felt crossed, as bitter emotions lay in the same bed with love and kindness. "Hang on, baby," Delta whispered in Megan's ear. "They're almost here. Don't even think about leaving me now. We . . . we haven't even played chess." Delta looked down at Megan and saw her crack open one swollen eye.

"Don't leave me," Megan forced through bloody lips.

Delta shook her head. "Not a chance. I haven't stood you up yet, have I?"

Megan tried to grin, but the pain stopped her. "You . . . won't . . . believe," Megan whispered, reaching her hand up to Delta.

"What?" Delta leaned closer to Megan's lips. "I won't believe what?"

Licking her cracked and torn lips, Megan groaned in pain. "The tattoo . . . he had the tattoo."

As Megan lapsed into unconsciousness, Delta cradled yet another battered loved one who had stepped in the way of the murderous blue machine.

As she gazed out into the dark, wet night outside, and the cold winter air anchored itself inside her, Delta calmly swallowed the anger stuck in her throat.

They had declared war on her.

And soon, they would feel her response.

24

Twitching herself awake, Delta quickly sat up in her chair. The harsh glare from the white hospital walls bounced like acid into her eyes, making her squint. Leaning over, Delta gazed down at the deeply sleeping Megan. She looked much better than when Delta got to her at the hotel. Her lips and cheek had been sewn up and the bump on her head had receded a bit, but the puffiness and bruises only worsened. Reaching out, Delta gently stroked Megan's face with the back of her hand. The knowledge that she wouldn't be in here if she didn't know Delta, burned like a brand on her heart. The disease was spreading to innocent people, and it was time to bring it to an end.

As Delta rose to stretch her stiff body, Megan stirred.

"Hi," Megan whispered, forcing a grin that crossed only half of her face.

"Hi, yourself," Delta answered, gently sitting on the side of the bed. "How're you feeling?" Taking Megan's bandaged hand, Delta lightly held it.

"Like a million bucks . . . that just went through a paper shredder. Oooh, my head is playing the drums."

Delta brought Megan's hand to her lips and kissed the back of it.

"You scared the shit out of me, you know."

Megan barely nodded. "Afraid you'd never have the chance to beat me at chess?" Megan's lips barely moved as she spoke.

Delta grinned. "Yeah, that too. But don't talk. I know it must hurt."

Megan's eyes filmed over. "Do I look like shit?"

Smiling at her tenacity, Delta nodded. "A little piece. The doctor said you have a concussion and some cracked bones, but you're still in one piece."

Megan smiled her half grin and turned to look out the window.

"What is it? What can I do?" Delta felt the sting of helplessness.

Looking back at Delta, Megan reached out and pulled her to her chest. "Hold me, please. Just hold me."

Wrapping her arms carefully around Megan's shoulders, Delta rocked her slowly, kissing her forehead.

After ten minutes, Megan pulled far enough away so she could see Delta's face.

"You don't need to tell me about it now," Delta offered softly.

Megan shook her head. "No one has ever been there for me like you were. I remember calling your name, and the next minute, you were beside me."

"I'm just glad I was there."

Megan squirmed a bit. "But I want to be here for you."

"Shhh. You are."

Megan shook her head again. "That's not what I mean. Del, they're after you. The guy who beat me up came looking for the matchbooks."

"What?"

"In between punches, he saw a book of matches on the table and grabbed them up. After he looked inside and found nothing, he swore, threw them on the floor, and started hitting me again."

"Is that all he was after?"

"No."

Delta pulled away to look her full in the face. "What is it?"

"I may not have had all my marbles in place, but I vaguely remember him warning me to keep my nose out of their business and to tell you the same."

Delta's blood froze. "Oh Megan, I never meant to—"

Megan pressed her fingers to Delta's lips. "Don't. Being with you these last few days have been the nicest in my life."

Delta winced. "But I shouldn't have asked you to get those names. I shouldn't have endangered you."

"Oh, I get it. You're the only one of us who gets to do that, is that it?"

"No, but—"

"But nothing. I want to be a part of your life, Delta, and if that means taking a few bumps and bruises along the way, then so be it." Wincing again, Megan lightly touched her torn lips.

Delta looked down at the bandaged hands and fought back the tears. "It shouldn't be this way."

"What shouldn't? Our love? Damn it, Delta, if we tried to follow all the rules, then arrest me now, because that's what rule number one would tell you to do."

Holding Megan tightly, Delta allowed a single tear to fall from her eye. "I never meant for you to get hurt."

"No, and you never meant to fall in love with a prostitute either. Things happen, Delta." Pushing Delta away so she could see her face, Megan brushed away the tear. "We happened. Are you sorry for that as well?"

"No. Never."

As much as it hurt to do so, Megan grinned. "Well that's good news. For a moment there I thought you might dump me."

Placing a kiss on Megan's good cheek, Delta sighed. "Not a chance."

Megan leaned back on the pillow and sighed heavily.

"I'd better let you get some rest."

Megan smiled, but her eyes were closed, and she was very pale.

Leaning over the bed, Delta kissed Megan's forehead. "I love you, Ms. Osbourne."

Megan grinned. "And I love you, Officer Stevens."

25

"How is she?"

Delta stepped through the door and into Connie's outstretched arms.

"She's a trooper."

Connie closed the door and escorted Delta to the kitchen and handed her a cup of coffee.

"Our tattooed killer, or someone wearing the same one, beat her up and warned us to stay out of it."

"Did she get a look at him?"

"No. He was wearing some kind of mask."

"They're after you now."

Plopping down in a chair, Delta rubbed her tight shoulders. "Yes, they are. Only I don't think they realize I'm not one to scare easily."

Connie stood behind Delta and rubbed her shoulders. "They must be tailing you. How else would they know about you and Megan?"

Delta closed her eyes and tried to relax her shoulders. "Could be they've bugged the phones. My guess is my inquiry into the missing dope. I'll bet that's got them scared."

Connie stopped rubbing Delta's shoulders and sat in front of her. "They could have killed her, you know."

Delta nodded. She didn't want to think about what could have happened. "It was a warning."

Connie tossed a folder over to Delta. "Think they warned Miles?"

"Hard to say. It's possible they threatened Jennifer and his kids. That would explain why he didn't say anything to me."

"Yes, it would. And if he felt his family was in danger, it would account for his dramatic change in attitude the last two weeks."

Delta's eyes narrowed. "You know there's no turning back."

Connie reached out and touched Delta's arm. "I never expected to."

"What did you and Eddie find out?"

"Well, there were eleven numbers to each series. Eddie divided them up in every possible way. This, of course, led us to one thousand, two hundred, and ten possibilities."

"Of course." Delta grinned. She couldn't balance her checkbook, let alone follow Connie's calculator-mind.

"Then, I punched in every possible number grouping relating to us — file numbers, car numbers, and, after you called, badge numbers. Once we did that, Eddie deleted your badge number from all the series."

"Give me an example. I'm not sure I follow."

Connie pointed to a number. "This number 73187875240. Does it look familiar?"

Delta stared at it. There was something distinctively familiar, but she couldn't place what it was.

Walking over to the computer at her desk, Connie motioned to the screen. "Now, Eddie takes out a badge number, which is a three digit number, and look what we end up with." Connie pressed return, sending the printer zipping back and forth. Tearing the paper out, Connie handed the results to Delta.

"See if you can't find a number on this list that means something to you."

Delta examined the list until her finger stopped at a number. The number was 73877540.

"That's the serial number of my gun."

"Exactly. The code combines serial numbers with badge numbers. Every third number is a badge number. Once Eddie deleted your badge number from all the numbers, we were left with a list of numbers eight numbers in length."

"But there's one digit too many. There is no zero in mine."

Connie exhaled loudly and took the paper from Delta. "My guess is that digit is the key to who is on the take, and who isn't. Take a look."

Taking the paper back, Delta studied all the numbers. The paper had two columns; one column had a list of serial numbers, and the other had the badge numbers opposite it. Looking at the serial numbers, Delta noticed that the final digit was either a one or a zero.

"Eddie also lifted the computed list of everyone's serial numbers. Gina and I cross-referenced it with badge numbers, and then it was a matter of me writing in who belonged to the badge numbers."

"You're amazing." Delta read the line of numbers.

"Look at your number, Miles's, and Hammond's numbers."

Delta looked at them. They all ended in zero. "Zeros are for the good guys, eh?"

Connie shrugged. "Or vice versa." Typing something into Eddie, Connie watched as the printer zipped back and forth once more. "There's more. Now let's take a look at the list of names on the evidence list." Connie tore the paper out of the printer and looked at it with Delta. "The week prior to Miles's death, it shows he went to the evidence room five times. Five. That's more times than you go in a month. And he wasn't admitting evidence either. I cross-referenced the dates to major busts and none of them match. What did match, was that Miles allegedly went every day right after a major drug bust. The pattern they've created is too obvious."

Delta nodded. "They've made it look as if he visits the evidence room after the admission of a lot of dope." Delta clenched her teeth together. "What about Hammond?"

"Notice that, while his name doesn't appear as frequently as Miles's does, it too, shows up at times other than when checking evidence."

"They've created the perfect scapegoat."

Connie nodded. "Yes, they have. If they do get caught, how easy it will be for them to blame it on the dead men."

Connie reached her arms around Delta's neck and pulled her closer. "I'm afraid for you, Storm."

Holding Connie tightly, Delta rocked a little. "It's not so bad, now that we know who's on our side."

Connie shook her head. "That's not why I'm scared. Look at the way the badge numbers line up."

Releasing Connie, Delta looked at the list and saw that the first badge number belonged to Miles, the second to Hammond and the third . . .

"What's this? A hit list?"

Connie nodded slowly. "I think so."

Delta looked down at the paper, up at Connie, and back to the paper. "What do you make of it?"

Connie reached over and laid her hand on top of Delta's. "I think we were wrong about the notebook. We've been assuming that these were Miles's codes. I'm betting they're not. Somehow, he must have discovered them during his initial investigation and was trying to decipher them himself."

Delta studied the numbers. A chilling numbness crept over her as she stared at the cold, inhuman numbers. "Where did Eddie have to go to get the serial numbers of our sidearms?"

Connie's eyes darkened. "We checked the Personnel files first, but they weren't there. Someone had erased them from Personnel's memory."

"Then what did you do?"

"What else? We busted into the system of our main suspect, and voilà, there they were."

"So . . ." Delta turned the paper over in her hand. "This is our Captain's own personal hit list?"

Connie nodded. "I'm afraid so. And if it is, you're next."

26

Pushing open the hospital door, Delta held a single red rose to Megan. "How you feeling?"

"You're so sweet, " Megan replied, taking the flower and smelling it. "I've felt better. How about you? You were pretty shaken up when you left."

"Seeing you like this isn't easy."

Megan patted the bed. "That's the first time anyone has ever told me I was hard to look at. Come here and tell me what we've got going so far."

Delta sat on the bed's edge and gently kissed Megan's cheeks and lips before explaining everything Connie and Eddie discovered.

"So your name is next on this list?" Megan reached for Delta's hand.

"It looks that way."

"It's not worth it, Del. There are probably hundreds more just like the ones in your crooked department. And even if you do catch them, there will be others after them."

Delta bowed her head. "Maybe so, but these particular ones killed Miles and beat you up. You just don't walk away from someone who does that to people you love, Meg. At least, I can't."

Megan's eyebrows joined in a frown. "No. You want to be like Miles and be carried away instead. You can't win, Delta. There's too many of them and not enough of you."

Delta sighed. "What would you have me do?"

Taking Delta's hand, Megan squeezed it between hers. "I just want to know that you're doing this for all the right reasons, and not for a bloodthirsty retribution or lofty law enforcement idealism."

Delta did not move her eyes from Megan's face. Didn't she understand it was that idealism that drew her to law in the first place. It was the idea of the satisfaction that came from helping people move more freely in a world filled with increasing lawless chaos.

Slowly pulling her hands from Megan's, Delta rose and went to the window. "I don't think you understand—"

"Why not? Because I come from the other side of the tracks? You're right. How can I possibly understand why you would continue to risk your life for a system that so obviously failed you?"

"Damn it, Megan, what do you want from me? Everything I believe in, everything I've loved and held dear, has been stripped away from me. I can't just pick up my things and walk out."

"What about your own life?"

Delta shook her head angrily. "My life wouldn't be worth much to me without my ideals or principles."

"Why not? Even if you succeed, where will that get you and your principles? You can't beat the system, Del."

Feeling the pain of anger and frustration well up inside her, Delta wheeled around. "Look, don't talk to me about a system you bailed out on long ago." The next hurtful word stuck deep in Delta's throat. "Oh God, Megan, " Delta said quietly, moving back over to the bed and taking her hand. "I'm sorry."

Megan held up her hand. "No, you're right. We live by two completely different set of rules. In your law-abiding world, everything is black or white, right or wrong, good or bad. My world is filled with a multitude of grays. We do what we have to do to survive, laws be damned. There's a world of difference between the two."

Sitting back on the bed, Delta still held Megan's hands. "So how is it we forged a bridge between the two?"

Megan smiled a crooked smile. "Would it sound too corny if I said love?"

Delta grinned. "Yes, but say it anyway." Leaning over, Delta gently kissed Megan.

Wrapping her arms around Delta, Megan held her close. "Just help me understand why you're so willing to put your life on the line for a system that has already turned its back on you and me both."

Stroking Megan's hair, Delta brushed her lips across Megan's bumpy forehead. "It has nothing to do with the fucked up system, I should be so gallant. It has to do with loyalty, with friendship."

Megan pulled slightly away. "Look, honey, don't get yourself blown off your white charger for this. Revenge has its price."

"A price you've already started paying for."

Megan lightly touched her bruised eye. "I've had worse, believe me."

Placing her hand on top of Megan's, Delta's finger ran over a bluing bump on the crest of her eyebrow. "When this is over, will you do something for me?"

"Name it."

"Will you come to Hawaii with me? Just the two of us? Let's take some time to enjoy what's happening between us?"

Megan's eyes danced. "I would love to. But only on one condition."

Delta nodded. "And that is?"

"You make love to me on the beach. I've always wanted to make love on the beach."

Nuzzling Megan's neck, Delta inhaled the fresh scent of her body. "You drive a hard bargain, but I think I can manage."

Pulling Delta closer, Megan squeezed her as tight as her aching body would allow. "There's one more thing I have to ask."

The serious tone of Megan's voice made Delta pull her head away from Megan's neck so they could face each other.

"You come back to me in one piece, Delta Stevens, because I didn't find you now, only to lose you because of some grand sense of loyalty. You understand?"

Looking into Megan's puffy face, Delta nodded. And, for the first time, she questioned her own motives.

27

Miles had been buried in the family plot next to his father, Captain David Brookman of the thirty-third precinct. Miles adored his father and had known ever since he was a child that he would follow in his footsteps. At twenty-one, Miles entered the Academy to take over where his father left off. And he did just that. Delta had often heard favorable comparisons of the two. If Miles Brookman followed the book, David Brookman wrote it.

Sitting next to Miles's headstone, Delta watched as the last light from the sun faded behind threatening clouds. Pulling her jacket snugly around her, Delta leaned closer to the headstone.

"I've always wondered if the dead could hear the living. Death just seems too final, and I don't think God is into such drastic endings. Maybe your spirit can hear me, Miles. I'd like to think that you can."

Pulling a tissue out from her pocket, Delta dabbed her eyes. "I miss you, big guy. So much has happened since you've been gone that sometimes I think I'll go mad." Delta inhaled jerkily. The air was cold and crisp, biting at the end of her nose.

"Maybe I have, and that's why I'm in a cemetery talking to a headstone. You were right when you said it was big. But I need to know . . . is it too big for me?" Delta paused, listening to her own question; feeling the sound of it inside her. "And I've come to a fork in the road where I have to make the decision to go on or get out of the department. I know which one you chose, but is that the best decision for me? We're two different people with two different needs. You lived for police work. Your badge was as vital to you as your heart. But I'm not like that. I'm a woman who's a cop, not a cop who's a woman. There's a big difference."

"I guess I need to know that I'm doing this for all the right reasons. As much as I desperately long to put Williams and his minions behind bars, getting myself killed in the process won't bring you back to life. If I'm going to ride this bucking bronco until it collapses, I need to know exactly why I'm doing it. Without that, I'm sure to get myself killed. I love you Miles, but I don't wish to join you, wherever that is."

Looking out across the street, Delta saw children swinging on swings in a tiny park as a woman watched over them. Standing by her truck, Delta peered out at the children as they squirmed and chattered to each other like magpies. The three of them couldn't have been more than four years old, and the smallest clutched onto a ragged brown teddy bear.

Suddenly, the sky broke open, heaving large drops upon the earth. The children squealed with delight and ran over to the woman who was now opening an aged umbrella. Gathering around her like chicks to a hen, they squeezed in to keep the rain from hitting them. Only the littlest one reached an arm out for the rain to land on. As she did this, her bear slipped out from under her arm, but the woman did not see it, and the little girl did not appear to notice.

As the woman opened the car door for the children, Delta ran across the street, picked up the bear, and jogged over to the woman who was closing the door.

"The little girl dropped this," Delta said, handing the bear to the woman.

"Oh, thank you. She would have carried on for days if she would have lost her bear. Thanks."

"No problem."

Still standing in the rain as the woman backed the car out of the park, Delta thought about Miles's children and the sadness etched in their faces as he was lowered into the ground. His little boy clutched tightly to a worn brown bear much like the one this little girl was carrying. Delta remembered that what hurt the most as Miles's coffin hit the ground was the realization that his little boy would never remember his daddy.

Closing her eyes, Delta pictured so clearly the little boy and his bear.

The answer she needed was there all along.

Bear. He would help.

28

When the front door swung open, a big, strapping, and overly hairy man stood smiling like a circus bear.

"Bear, it's so good to see you." Delta stepped into the hallway and hugged him. Her arms barely circled his waist.

"You too, Del. What's up?"

Delta sat down on the small flowery couch in the den. Bear's home was cozy and made even more comfortable by the fire burning steadily in the brick fireplace. On the wall were several pictures of Bear and his friends from the CHP, most of whom were motorcycle cops. There was also a picture from the Police Academy with Bear hugging Miles. The pictures hung crookedly over a mantelpiece scattered with miniature cars. Even with Lynn's feminine touches, the house felt like the home of a cop.

"I wish this were a pleasure call, but I'm afraid it isn't."

Bear nodded and sat across from Delta on a large, aging rocker. "I didn't suspect it was."

Inhaling, Delta took the plunge. "I need your help."

Bear did not move. He didn't even blink.

"God, Bear, I don't even know where to begin."

Suddenly, Bear stood up. "Wait a second. Maybe I've got something that will help." Bear walked out of the room but was back in seconds, holding a small envelope. "I suppose this has to do with Miles's death?"

Delta's jaw dropped open. He knew. "How did you—"

Holding his hand up, Bear stopped her. "I don't know anything, Del, really. All I can tell you is Miles came here two days before he was shot and told me to give you this envelope only if you came looking for it."

"What?" Delta felt a zinger run wickedly up her spine.

Bear shrugged and handed Delta the envelope. "He said if anything should happen to him, that he wanted me to give this to you. He asked me to ask no questions, so I didn't."

Delta feverishly opened the envelope. Inside, were report numbers of drug-related busts followed by the amount of dope entered in the report and the actual amount of dope in evidence. In all, there were seven report numbers listed, along with the reporting officers and the number of pounds of dope missing from the evidence room.

Looking up at Bear, Delta smiled softly. "Did you know I'd come?"

Bear nodded. "Eventually."

"How?"

"He knew you too well. Miles must have known you'd end up here sooner or later. I just hope that whatever's in that envelope helps you nail who did it."

"And you really don't know what's in here?"

Shaking his head, Bear grinned. "If Miles wanted me to know what was going on, he would have told me. But he didn't."

Delta stared down into the envelope. He knew. He knew she wouldn't let go. He expected her to go after them. "Did he say anything else?"

"Nope. I asked him what he was up to, and all he would say was that it was something big." Bear leaned closer to Delta and lowered his voice. "It is, isn't it?"

Delta nodded her head slightly. "It sure is."

"Did it get him killed?"

Delta nodded again.

"If you need anything from me Delta, just name it. I don't need to know the particulars. If you find out who offed Miles, I'll help in anyway I can. All you have to do is call."

Delta took one of his hairy paws in her hand. "That means a lot to me, Bear. You can't imagine how alone I've felt since he died."

"Well Darlin', I'm here. Don't hesitate to pick up the phone."

Rising to leave, Delta looked once more at the picture of Bear and Miles. "He trusted you a lot, Bear."

"Yes, he did. And I trust that whatever was going down was important enough for him to risk his life over. Nail the bastards, Del."

"That's the plan."

Starting down the wet pavement, Delta whispered to herself, "That's exactly what I'm going to do."

29

Connie sat at Eddie II, her home computer, and pounded madly at the keys. The sole matchbook lay on the table next to the keyboard, and Delta sat backwards in a chair with her arms dangling over the back. She had raced back to Connie's with the remainder of Miles's report, talking a streak and gesticulating wildly. She had what she needed now to get the game rolling.

"Although there's no code to break on this one, it's going to take a while to match all the patrol units with their occupants who were driving them on these certain days." Connie pressed return and Eddie II hummed.

"The way I see it, we have less than forty hours before I go back to work. Until then, I don't have to worry about them coming after me. They won't touch me until I get back on duty."

"Do you think they'll strike the first night you go back?"

Delta nodded. "I want to force their hand. If we make them nervous, they've got to come after me. We're better off knowing when they're coming. That's our most important move. We must make them think I'm this close to nailing them."

Connie nodded and turned back to the computer. "So far, it looks as if they got in as many different patrol cars as possible. God, can you believe they delivered their dope in their own units? Talk about moxy."

Delta cracked a walnut and popped the meat in her mouth. "They're just like any other criminal who believes they won't get caught. After a while, they get sloppy."

"Miles must have stepped in some of their slop."

Delta nodded. "We won't make the same mistakes. Miles didn't know when they were coming, but we will." Delta gazed into the monochrome monitor. Visions of Megan's battered face floated before her. They had actually declared war on Delta and the people in her life. They were fools for believing that she could be scared away; especially now.

Delta suddenly rose from the chair. "I've got to get Megan out of the hospital."

"You think they'd really go after her in there?"

"They may underestimate us, but I won't do the same. I want to know she's safe."

"Then bring her over here. If they're tailing you, she won't be safe at your place either. I think we'd all be better off staying here until this thing is over. You know, strength in numbers and all that."

Delta smiled and placed her hand on Connie's shoulder. "You're the best."

"Yeah, well, so are you. So now what?"

"Once you and Eddie find out which cops are delivering to the Red Carpet, then we're set."

Connie turned from Eddie. There were streaks of gray in her black hair that Delta hadn't noticed before. "Do you think they would just go on killing?"

Feeling worn and tired, Delta shrugged. "Miles came too close, that's all. I'm sure they didn't want to kill him, but Miles and Hammond were threats. Like common criminals, eliminating threats comes naturally."

Connie reached over and touched Delta's hand. "You're their biggest threat now, Storm."

"Yes," Delta said, smiling. "That I am."

30

"Are you sure you don't mind me staying here?"

"Wouldn't have it any other way," Gina said, fluffing up a pillow and placing it behind Megan's back. "Delta won't rest until she knows you're safe. You'll be safe here. Those two Dobermans in the back won't let anyone within twenty yards of the house."

Megan looked over at the doorway where Delta stood listening.

"How are you feeling?" Delta asked, stepping into the light blue bedroom.

"About as good as any woman might feel after being rushed out of the hospital."

Delta leaned over and kissed her playfully on the nose. "Admit it — you loved it."

Megan smiled her new crooked grin. "'Yes, I guess I did. And . . .'" Lightly touching Delta's cheek, Megan brought it to her and brushed her lips across it. "I love you for it."

Delta felt herself blush as Gina quietly left the room.

"Do you really have to go through with this?"

Sitting on the side of the bed, Delta took one of Megan's hands. "I'm afraid so. If there was a safer way, we'd do it. I can promise you that."

Megan opened her arms to Delta, who leaned back into the embrace. "You go to work in ten hours."

Delta nodded. "That gives us ten hours to play with."

"You're playing with your life."

Delta gently squeezed Megan's hand. "Trust that I won't do anything foolish, Meg."

"What happens if Connie can't pinpoint the rest of the bastards before you go on?"

"Then I do everything I can to take my would-be assassin alive, so we can squeeze him. Once I have one of them, I'll get him to squeal like a pig. That's the one thing all criminals have in common; they never take the fall alone. Dirty cops are no exception."

Megan exhaled loudly. "It all scares the shit out of me. The thought of you out there with people you're supposed to trust, hunting you, trying to murder you like an animal makes me sick."

"Then wouldn't you rather that I go after them, instead of always watching my ass?"

Megan turned her face from Delta. "I suppose."

Delta lightly touched Megan's arm. "Megan, we're dealing with desperate people here. Do you really think they would let me live even if I quit? I know too much, and after today, they're scared to death of me."

Megan turned back to face her. "What do mean? What did you do today?"

Delta rose from the bed and paced over to the window. "I went in to work and snooped around the files and the evidence room. I asked a lot of questions of a lot of people and also put in a requisition for some bugging equipment. I've made my presence well known, and by now, they know I'm this close." Delta held her thumb and index finger together. "It's their move."

"What do you want with bugging equipment?"

"I may need to get some confessions on tape." I sure as hell don't want to be out on that street alone."

"Is that admissible in court?"

Delta shrugged. "Sometimes it is, sometimes it isn't. But I don't want their confessions as much as I want them to name the big man."

"And after that?"

"Then we go after him."

"And after you've put them all behind bars?"

Delta gently ran her fingers through Megan's hair. "Then it's just you and me."

Megan reached out and pulled Delta back to the bed. "Do we have to wait that long? Or am I horrible to look at with my puffy face and black eyes?"

"You are always beautiful to me, Megan Osbourne." Carefully climbing on the bed, Delta straddled Megan until she was sitting on her thighs. Megan's cleavage appeared cavernous beneath the low cut negligee and Delta envisioned burying her face there and never coming up for air.

"You must really love me, Delta, because I've seen what I look like, and it's not a pleasant sight. I make Freddy look like a sweet fairy prince."

Slowly unbuttoning the plum negligee she had bought for Megan, Delta slid both hands under her breasts and tenderly cupped them. "I do love you, Meg," she said, kissing the bumps and scars already forming on her eyebrows.

As she played with the hard nipples and rolled them around in her fingers, Delta bit tenderly Megan's neck and shoulders. Megan always tasted like she just walked out of a shower, and the clean smell drove Delta crazy.

Sliding down so she lay on top of Megan, Delta looked lovingly into the ice-blue eyes sparkling up at her, longing for her. "And tonight, I'm going to show you just how much."

31

Delta stepped behind Connie and watched as her fingers rapidly skimmed over the keyboard. She could tell by the way she pounded at the keys that Connie was anxious about uncovering the main man before Delta went back to work.

"Relax a little, will you?" Laying her hands on Connie's shoulders, Delta massaged them. "You're pretty tight."

"Uptight is more like it. Damn, Delta, I've scoured every possible corner, and I can't come up with anything that would be a conclusive link to Williams."

Sitting next to Connie, Delta grinned at Gina, who sat reading on the couch. "What does your gut tell you?"

Turning slowly from the monitor, Connie inhaled deeply before answering. "Gut?"

"Gut."

Connie licked her lips. "I'd have to go with either Captain Williams or Trask. Those are the only two who have access to both the files and the dope. I lean more toward Williams because of the new change in evidence room policies and the fact that his computer files have the serial numbers, and I couldn't locate them anywhere."

"You don't think anyone else can get in the way you did?" Connie drew back in mock surprise. "Are you kidding? Most of the guys in the department don't even know how to turn a computer on, let alone gain entry into someone else's locked system."

This made Delta smile. "Then how do you explain Miles's name being entered twice on days he wasn't in town? Don't you think one of the evidence cronies could have punched it in?"

Connie nodded. "I thought of that. It's entirely possible that one of them is in on it, but certainly wouldn't be the main man. That's why I lean more toward Williams. The man is a total pig. When is the last time you saw him on the streets? I swear, he's become a permanent fixture in that office."

"That's not enough to hang the man."

"No, but with the evidence list, the serial numbers, the fact that Larson's report was shot through, should be enough to raise someone's eyebrows."

Delta tossed the paper back on the table. "It's still not enough. I'm going to have to get someone to say his name on tape."

Connie took her wad of gum out and tossed it into the trash. "God that makes me nervous."

Delta shrugged. "I never really thought there was any other way."

Connie turned to Delta, her eyebrows scrunched in a deep frown. "I don't want you out there alone. Isn't there someone we can trust to watch your backside?"

Delta smiled. "There is."

"Who?"

"Bear."

"Bear? He's not even in our department."

"Exactly."

"Does he know?"

"He knows that Miles was killed during some kind of investigation, but that's about all. He told me to call him if I needed him."

"You need him."

"Can you link up with the computer in his unit?"

"No problem."

"Great. Using Eddie, you two can keep in contact during my shift. If anything goes sour, you can call him to come bail me out."

Connie sighed. "I feel a little better knowing we have at least one friend out there."

Delta agreed. "I think I'd better get some sleep. Tonight may be the longest night of my life."

Connie turned from the monitor and looked up at Delta. "I wish I were going out there with you."

Patting the top of the monitor, Delta grinned. "You will be. You think you have everything you need for tonight?"

Connie inhaled and nodded. "Gina and I are all set. How's your end?"

Delta ran her hand through her hair. It was hard to believe that in less than twenty-four hours, it would all be over.

"I'm ready. First move is the black knight's. After that, they're ours."

32

Delta studied herself carefully in the full-length mirror hanging in Connie's guest bathroom. She looked more different than she'd ever seen herself; there was an agedness, a sort of wisdom in her eyes that she hadn't remembered seeing before. Perhaps it was just fatigue — exhaustion from the mental chase she'd been on since Miles died; fatigue from battling grotesque emotions threatening to break her spirit and corrupt everything she believed in. She had closed herself off from these emotions, afraid they would entrench themselves so deep within her that she would back away from the only course of action open to her.

Delta admitted she was afraid. Fear was one emotion that kept cops from making stupid mistakes. Fearing the unknown, fearing the enemy is one thing, but being afraid of a friend was a different sort of fear altogether. With an enemy, she'd never let her guard down — she didn't worry about looking over her shoulder because she never turned her back. This was a new game, and Delta didn't know all the rules.

Maybe there weren't any. Or maybe, for the first time ever, she understood the multitude of grays Megan had talked about.

Thus far, the media and the public believed there were cop killers on the loose. Every law enforcement agency within one hundred miles were on the look out for that damned van with a tattooed man inside. Delta hated thinking about the manpower exerted in tracking down the fictitious felon. Cops everywhere were drawing their weapons on every suspicious action or movement. An almost irrational panic swept over everyone wearing a badge. These killers had done so much more than cheat the system; they were responsible for at least two deaths and innumerable drug-related crimes. Delta would see to it that they paid dearly.

Turning from the mirror, Delta walked into the bedroom, where Megan sat reading a textbook from one of her classes.

"You're sure this guy Bear will be there for you?" Megan asked, letting the book fall in her lap.

Delta sat on the edge of the bed, and her bulletproof vest hiked up so she adjusted it. "I sure hope so."

Megan held her hand. "Scared?"

"Shitless." Delta could feel her pulse pounding at her temples.

"Is that a good thing or a bad thing?"

This made Delta grin. "It's a good thing. Fear keeps you on your toes." Sitting next to Megan, Delta leaned into her embrace. "It's strange. The thing I'm afraid of most is that, after tonight, I may never work in law enforcement again."

"Why not? If you stop them, you should be given a medal or something."

Delta suppressed a grin. "Megan, even good cops don't like snitches. Cops are a lot like politicians and professional athletes: we feel we're not only above the law but that we should be allowed to handle everything in-house."

"I see. So what you're saying is, even though you do an incredible job, you'll be ostracized nonetheless."

Delta felt a pinprick in her heart. "Something like that. You never can tell. If we get no support from the masses, I'll be forced to give up police work."

"That would kill you, wouldn't it?"

Delta shook her head. "No, what would kill me would be to walk away. I can handle it if I give this everything I have and still have to leave. At least I'll know I gave it my best shot."

"That's important to you, isn't it? Doing right by people."

Delta nodded.

"What must you think of me then?"

Kissing the top of Megan's head, Delta hugged her tightly. "I think you're the greatest thing that's happened to me in a long time. I don't care what you do for a living or what you've had to do in the past. I think I'm beginning to understand something about those gray colors you were telling me about."

"Really?"

"Really."

"I wish I could say the same about your world. I don't think I'll ever really understand."

Turning into Megan's embrace, Delta kissed her hard. "It's not important that we understand what we do as long as we love and understand who we are."

"And you really believe that?"

"With everything I've got."

For a moment, the two women looked into each other's eyes, speaking without words, and feeling without touch. Slowly, their faces moved closer until their lips parted and met, barely touching, yet feeling that loving warmth. Gently pulling Megan to her, Delta wrapped her arms around Megan's tiny waist and kissed her softly. It was as if the softer they kissed, the more they shared.

Slowly removing her lips from Megan's, Delta kissed her nose and chin. "I do love you, Megan Osbourne."

Megan smiled. "Then come back to me, Delta Stevens. Come back and take me to Hawaii like you promised."

Standing to leave, Delta looked at Megan one last time. "And we know I would never stand a beautiful woman up." Kissing Megan's forehead, Delta started for the door. "And you make sure Gina and the dogs are ready on time."

Megan's eyes twinkled. "In prostitute school, we learned that timing is everything. We won't let you down."

Closing the bedroom door behind her, Delta smiled and shook her head.

Prostitute school?

33

Connie was already at work when Delta arrived. She was furiously entering data into Eddie when Delta pulled a chair up next to her.

"Well?"

Connie did not look up. "We're in."

"Bear didn't ask any questions?"

"Not one. He just said what you told me he'd say; that if you needed him, he'd be there."

Delta sighed. "Great."

"Are you expecting them to roll over right away?"

Delta nodded. "But I can't bring them here. Once they start talking, I'll have to take them to the county jail. If they get back here, we're doomed."

"Agreed. What are you going to do about your less-than-illustrious partner?"

"I'll have to feel him out first. It sure would be nice to know he was on our side, wouldn't it?"

Connie nodded. "I sure would feel better knowing that both of you were looking for the bullet." Connie looked up from the monitor. "How's Megan taking all this?"

"I can't really expect her to understand it all. I'm not so sure I understand it all myself."

Connie looked back at the monitor and lowered her voice. "She adores you, you know."

"I know."

"And from the looks of it, you're pretty stuck on her, aren't you?" Delta felt herself warm. "She's unlike anyone I've ever met. There are so many facets to her, it would take a lifetime to get to know them all."

"I hope you have that long, Storm. I really do."

Delta grinned and threw her arms around Connie. She no longer cared who saw. Tonight was her night. "Thanks."

Reaching down to touch Delta's knee, Connie continued. "I'll be listening to every sound you make out there."

Delta glanced over at the portable AM-FM radio sitting on Connie's desk. It appeared to be a typical radio-cassette, but inside, there was a CB radio locked in on the dispatcher's frequency. A small thin earphone traveled down the floor and the ear plug at the end lay neatly coiled on the desk. It was an invention Connie rigged up years ago when one of the officers was a lover of hers. The CB enabled her to listen to the kinds of calls her lover was being sent to while she was working. She hadn't used it in years.

"I feel better already." Checking her watch, Delta waved to Taggart as he walked through the back entrance.

"You ready?" Connie asked, squeezing Delta's hand.

Delta nodded. "I'm wired, and I have one for him when I catch him. I'll put it on him the moment I've got his ass. Then we'll let him hang himself and anyone else."

".Just don't get fancy. If he doesn't talk, get him to the jail and don't mess with it. He'll confess sooner or later. You just need to get off the street as soon as possible. Lord knows, if they're desperate enough, you might take a cop's slug in the back."

Delta nodded, feeling the cold creep up her arms.

Connie turned from the monitor, her face grim and unsmiling. "Don't take any unnecessary risks out there. Being a dead hero won't do anyone any good."

Delta shook her head. "I'll be more than careful, don't worry." Adjusting her vest, Delta stared at the monitor. The weight from her vest felt like the weight of the world.

"Keep your holster unlocked and your wits about you. If anything starts turning sour, bail out."

Smiling warmly into her friend's face, Delta patted the monitor. "You and Eddie and your little gizmo there should keep me safe for a while." Looking down into the concerned eyes, Delta lightly touched Connie's cheek. "I couldn't have done any of this without you."

"Thank me when you walk through that door at the end of your shift." Taking Delta's hand, Connie kissed the back of it. "Be very, very careful, my friend, and come home safely."

Walking away from Connie and past the tinted glass of the Captain's office, Delta gritted her teeth.

Gripping the door knob to his office, Delta gagged back the bitterness rising in her throat. Captain Williams looked up from the dim desk light, his face blank.

"I just wanted you to know, sir," Delta hesitated after heavy emphasis on the word, 'sir.' "That I WILL see you when this shift is over."

Captain Williams's only movement was the raising of one eyebrow.

"There just aren't enough people in the world, sir, capable of keeping me from bringing Miles's killer to justice. And rest assured — that's exactly what I'm going to do." Closing the door behind her, Delta started off for the bathroom, feeling the bitterness transform into anger. He would not do to her what he had done to her partner.

Once in the bathroom, Delta double-checked the wires taped to her vest. Her heart pounded hard inside her chest, and her palms were already sweating. She wondered if Captain Williams was standing outside waiting for her. She wondered whether or not he was the least bit scared of her. She wondered . . .

Pulling Miles's badge out of her bag, Delta stared at it. "This is it, pal," Delta whispered, shining the badge with her shirt sleeve. "It's game time." Dropping his badge into her left chest pocket, Delta buttoned it and took one last look in the mirror. Her eyes were small and hard, and her eyebrows formed a nasty frown. Delta looked and felt like a warrior off to battle. Yes, it was game time, and this time, they would play for keeps.

34

In the muster room, Taggart handed Delta a radio and her baton. "I got here a little early, so I fished out our toys."

Delta took the radio and set it in the holder on her belt. The baton she held in her hands until muster was over. Throughout the entire room, Delta's eyes moved from officer to officer, trying to get a read on anyone acting suspicious or nervous. But the squadroom had been uptight since the two deaths, and Delta knew she would not be able to tell simply by looking. No, only by acting would she bring them down.

When muster was finally over, Delta and Taggart made their way to their unit.

"How were your days off?" He asked as they buckled their seat belts.

"Interesting. I discovered a great deal about Miles's death." Delta threw this out early.

Taggart looked at her sideways. "What are you talking about?"

Delta turned the radio down. "You know what I'm talking about. You know why Miles was killed." It was a wild stab, but she didn't have time for guessing games.

Taggart's face turned white. "But—"

"No. No buts. You've known about the selling of confiscated dope for a while now, haven't you?"

Taggart said nothing.

"What you may not know is that there's a list of who's who, and you and I are on it."

"What do you mean, a list?"

"You know, a hit list."

"Be serious, Stevens."

"Look, all I know is that our names are the next on the list. Don't play dumb with me, Taggart. Our lives are in danger, and you know it."

Taggart started the car and nodded slowly. "Yes, yes I do."

"I've been making a lot of people uncomfortable with my snooping around, just like Miles did. They'll have to come after me tonight because they know I could nail them anytime."

Taggart nodded again. "I hear you."

Delta carefully examined Taggart's every expression. "What have you done to make them want your ass on a cement platter?"

Taggart slowed for a red light and turned to Delta. "I walked in on them one night when Larson and Owens were loading the dope. They gave me some half-baked story about shipping it to another station, but I could tell something wasn't right. Since then, I've been running scared. I didn't know who to trust."

For the next half-hour, both officers were silent as they looked out over the dark, shadowy landscape of the beat. Only the crackle of the radio returned them from their secret thoughts.

"S1012, there's a 602 and possible 459 in progress at 600 North Hemingway. Neighbors believe suspect has already left the scene. Proceed with caution. S1019 will backup if necessary."

Backup would be Patterson and McKlinton. The trap was beginning to spring.

Taggart glanced over at Delta before switching on the lights. "And we're off."

Delta stared at Taggart for a long moment. Something didn't feel right. There was something unfamiliar about his demeanor that bothered her. Maybe he wasn't taking this seriously enough. Or maybe he was just too cool under the circumstances. Whatever it was, it raised the hackles on her neck.

Only now, it was too late. The black knight had played, and it was her move.

35

Slowing up to the south side of North Hemingway, Taggart shut the engine off.

"What do you think?"

Delta squinted into the darkness. One lone streetlight shone down on the street in front of them, illuminating the large parking lot and back alley. By her calculations, there were innumerable ways for someone on foot to escape once they exited the warehouse. The key would be to drive them out from wherever they came. She and Miles had been successful at that over a dozen times. For whatever reason, most burglars didn't have brains enough to bolt out the front door. Instead, most made haste toward the only sure exit; the one they'd created in the first place.

As Delta continued her visual surveyance of the area, the radio crackled: neighbors heard what sounded like glass breaking prior to seeing a flash of light from the interior.

Delta glanced over at Taggart. His face was uncharacteristically wrinkled in a frown.

"Let's check the west windows first," he offered, pulling the keys from the ignition.

Delta agreed. Reaching for the shotgun, Delta also grabbed two additional rounds and dropped them in her right chest pocket.

"Geez, Stevens, what're you gonna do with that thing?"

Delta flicked off the safety switch. "The last time I didn't take the shotgun, my partner was killed. Would you rather I left it?"

Taggart did not answer. "What about your flashlight?" he asked, dropping his six-cell into its holder.

"We can use yours if you want. I don't like them. All they're good for is announcing to the scum where you are. I like it better when the odds are in my favor."

Shrugging his shoulders, Taggart mumbled to himself, "That Brookman sure taught you some weird shit."

Carefully moving to the east side, Delta heard glass crunch at her feet. Instantly, she and Taggart were against the wall. As the noise ceased, Taggart shined his flashlight on the ground and saw shards of broken glass laying at their feet.

Delta stooped down, looked at the glass, and then back at the window. The window was barely above her eye-level, which wasn't odd considering the age of the building. More than likely, she thought, the window was to the basement of the building, which extended beneath street level.

As Taggart moved over to the window, he signaled to her that he was going around to check other possible entry points.

In less than one minute, Taggart returned shaking his head and holding up one finger. This was the only point of entry, so they, too, would enter here.

Watching Taggart signal again, Delta nodded slowly. The dark around them was so thick, it felt tangible upon her body. Handing Taggart the shotgun, Delta pulled herself up to the window, swung her legs over, and jumped down amid more broken glass. Fearful that the noise would alert the intruder, Delta dove, rolled, and ducked behind a steel girder. She had been right about the floor being beneath street level; the drop was almost twice that of the initial climb.

Peering through the black hole of a warehouse, Delta could barely see a thing. She was enshrouded by blackness that must have been the length of a football field, but was approximately less than half its width. Still, Delta could see it was a large building with outlines of boxes and crates scattered all around. The ceiling extended well over thirty feet, and Delta thought she could make out scaffolds ringing the entire room. She and Miles had been in an old warehouse such as this once. She remembered him telling her that scaffolding was the old way that warehouses had to stack boxes and crates.

As her eyes adjusted to the darkness, Delta could faintly make out a giant forklift in one corner and other pieces of machinery in the other. There was a maze of cartons, boxes, scaffolding, and machinery — the worst possible layout. He could be anywhere. If her memory served her right, this warehouse had nothing but paper products and fig bars. The arson potential was extremely high, and Delta immediately started looking at the other windows for other ways out. One of her greatest fears as a child was burning to death. Since then, she always walked into a room scanning for every possible exit.

Suddenly, the streamline of the shotgun caught her eye, and she reached out and grabbed it from Taggart.

"Go," he whispered, "outside."

Delta knew this meant he wanted her to circle along the outside perimeter of the interior. He would follow, covering her rear.

As she made her way around the large wooden crate, Delta stepped into one of the anterooms on either side of the warehouse. There was a stillness in this area that gripped her like frozen wind.

"Taggart?" she whispered, breaking the rules of search procedure. But, if she broke them, Taggart didn't. He said nothing.

Squinting in the darkness, Delta heard the crackling noise behind her. Whirling in the dark, the shotgun hit something sticking out and clattered to the ground. Picking it up, Delta took five steps and peered around the corner to view the entry way. No one was in sight; and neither was Taggart. He must have taken a farther position from her than what she was used to. Miles used to get right up her backside. She always felt safe knowing he was watching her back.

Delta turned to continue on, but something made her turn back to the window. She should get out. Why should she risk her life over some dumb fig bars? Besides, without Taggart in view, they were now in danger of shooting each other. Where had he gone? Weighing her options, Delta decided that retreat was the smarter maneuver.

Squatting down with her back pressed against the wall, Delta hugged the shotgun close to her, her finger resting on the trigger. She did not like the feel of this at all. Where in the hell was Taggart? She wanted to call for him again, but didn't want to jeopardize her position. Her heart raged in her ears, and sweat sat in neat beads on her upper lip. Why hadn't he at least signaled her with that damned flashlight? Inching her way under another window, Delta felt a panic grip her. Taggart hadn't told her that all the other doors and windows were barred. If this was an arson job, she and the arsonist would be fighting for the same exit. If it was her hit, she was trapped with only one way out.

Delta was going to count to three and make a run for the broken window, but just before she got to two, large crates toppled over, landing in her path and crunching the remains of the window pieces on the floor. If she hadn't jumped back, the boxes would have crushed her as well.

Squatting behind a steel girder, Delta reached deep for her wits. Something was terribly wrong, and if the windows weren't barred, she would have gone right through one. Squatting even lower, Delta listened.

There's a different sound to a peaceful silence and a foreboding one. The silence prior to an earthquake is one that pricks up the ears of animals and leaves a heavy shadow upon the land. The silence of the forest in winter leaves a serene taste of calm to all who listen. As Delta listened to the quiet, she knew she was hearing the foreboding silence warning her to be careful; telling her that this wasn't an arson job, or a robbery. In that instant, in that one-millionth of a second, she felt Miles reach out and touch her.

This was it.

Licking her pursed lips, Delta turned away from the point of entry and moved back to the anteroom. The game was afoot, and now, she need not be afraid. Surely, they anticipated her to panic like a trapped animal and force her way through the sole exit. But panic was not her style. They counted on her to act "like a woman," but they were way off.

They were playing her game now, and what they didn't know about Delta was that she did not know how to lose.

Cutting back across the warehouse, carefully avoiding the moonlight maze dancing on the floor and walls, Delta hesitated. That same cold chill she felt earlier swept over her. Leaning against the crates, Delta heard heavy footsteps crunch across the glass as the boxes were being pushed aside. Maybe the crates had landed on Taggart. Maybe they weren't meant for her. Delta swallowed hard. Maybe they were taking them both out right now. Whatever the case, they had done the one thing she had counted on them to do: they had severely underestimated her.

Moving slowly through the darkness, Delta felt no fear; only a cold, hard determination to push justice through the eye of a needle.

Feeling the bead of sweat roll down her back, Delta wanted to take off her jacket, but afraid too much movement would alert her hunter to her position. Afterall, it was so dark in there, he could be feet from her, and she might not know it.

As the crunching of the glass ceased, Delta rested the butt of the shotgun on her left shoulder. Its weight was a comfort to her now as she held it straight up toward the ceiling. She knew she could lower it in the blink of an eye and blast a gaping hole through a watermelon before most people could say "Bang!"

Looking around, Delta was not happy with her present position. She needed a vantage point — a place where she was in control and could see more. Right now, she felt like a rat in a maze, and she needed to be free. Eyeing the scaffold, Delta started her tedious journey across the cement floor.

Just as she reached the stairs, Delta heard her company bang into a box, and he cursed under his breath. He was somewhere between one and four o'clock to her left, and about twenty-five feet away. Looking up at the scaffold, she realized much of it was bathed in moonlight; too risky. She would have to make her stand someplace darker. If he continued moving toward her, his silhouetted figure against the window would come into full view. This would give her the best shot open to her.

Lowering the barrel, Delta closed one eye and took sight of the window with the other. She realized now that her hunter was not a cop, he had made too many tactical mistakes in a warehouse situation to have ever been a cop. If he was, he would never allow himself to walk right in front of the far window, no matter how dark it was. And as his soft-soled shoes moved closer to her, Delta was sure he'd end up in front of the window.

Putting slight pressure on the trigger, Delta barely breathed. The pounding of her heart had slowed, but the beating still resounded in her ears. One, two, maybe three more seconds, and he would come into her sights. There was no time for regret or guilt. It was self-preservation, and she had no compunction about blowing his head off his shoulders.

Suddenly, a large-framed outline appeared in her sights. With slow, deliberate hesitation, Delta breathed in, held it, and depressed her finger evenly on the trigger.

Instead of a reverberating bang and thunderous kick, only a loud, ominous, empty click echoed through the warehouse. For a second, Delta stared at the gun in disbelief as it lay in her hands, cold and empty.

In the second that followed, a booming roar and flash of light exploded, lifting her off her feet and throwing her backward against the crates. The light from the gun flash temporarily blinded her as she crashed, sending the useless shotgun clattering once more across the floor.

As the light spots left her eyes, Delta saw the outline slowly move toward her. Grabbing the left side of her chest, Delta rolled, withdrew her weapon, and crawled beneath the raised forklift.

Her chest was on fire, and she felt dazed and confused. Her left side was throbbing in unison with her pounding heart. Delta painfully scooted over to the other side of the forklift. Every move she made drove a sharp spike through her shoulder as she inched into the darker area beneath the forklift.

Looking back at the window, the apparition was gone. As her eyes readjusted to the minimal light, she saw the barrel of the shotgun gleaming in the night. Delta knew she stood a better chance against him with the shotgun than with her pea-shooter, so she reached across the floor and painfully pulled it to her. Her left chest continued to burn, and it felt as if she'd been stabbed with a hot poker. When she reached up with her right hand to feel blood, Delta didn't find any. The blood must not have soaked through her vest yet, she mused, wincing.

Pulling the shotgun to her, Delta opened it. The gun hadn't, as she originally thought, misfired. It had been emptied of its rounds; emptied, she surmised, when she handed it to Taggart. That was why it took him a little longer to follow her through the window; he was unloading her weapon. She remembered his reaction to her wanting to bring it along.

Damn him, she thought angrily. Damn them all.

But she was not beaten. Delta reached in her right pocket and pulled out the two rounds she'd brought along and loaded them into the empty chamber. So, Taggart had brought her here to die, did he? Slowly slipping the radio out from its holder, Delta knew it was time to call in the reinforcements. Once she announced that S1012 was in need of assistance, Connie would have Bear there in an instant.

Pulling the radio out, Delta also pulled her sidearm. She knew that the noise from the radio would alert him to her position, but she had to take that chance.

As Delta turned the radio on, she waited for the usual crackle and hum. Instead, the radio was silent. Turning the volume up, and still hearing nothing, Delta realized she had been burned once more, by Taggart. She remembered him offering her the radio after he came in early to "get their toys."

She may not have a radio, but she had one piece left to play.

Pushing the shotgun ahead of her, Delta made the biggest gamble of her life. She remembered once, when she and Connie were playing chess, Connie told her that sometimes the best move was the most preposterous, illogical, and outlandish move one could make. She told her that unpredictability was often a chess player's greatest ally. Connie had beaten her and Miles on several occasions because of that very strategy.

Scooting out from under the forklift, Delta felt along the wall. Her left hand held the gun while her right hand crept along, searching, feeling, until finally touching the light switch. Inhaling, wiping her right palm on her pants, Delta lowered the shotgun, backed her shoulder underneath the light switch, and held her breath.

Delta pressed up against the light switch and then back down again. The flash of light was harsh and unyielding, but was on long enough for her to see her prey standing watch by the broken window. Without a second's hesitation, Delta lowered the shotgun and squeezed the trigger as a thunderous clap filled the warehouse. In the darkness, she watched the body rise up, and before it could land, she pressed the trigger once more, sending the dark figure crashing against the fallen crates before slumping to the floor. Discharging, Delta moved over to the body.

"Turn over, you son of a bitch," Delta growled, withdrawing her sidearm and pointing it at the back of his head. A broad beam of moonlight made its way across the still body.

Still aiming her gun, Delta turned the body over with her foot. Blood trickled out of hundreds of tiny pellet holes in his chest, arms, neck, and face. Delta's aim was unerring.

Dropping the shotgun on the ground, Delta steadied her weapon on the face of the dead man. At once, she wanted to empty her weapon into his mouth. She wanted to kick him for both killing and forcing her to kill him. She hated his bloodied corpse and everything it stood for. She hated him for what he had done to Megan, for how he brutally and coldly beat her senseless. She hated him for the way he calculatingly killed Miles in cold blood that night. He was a killing machine and now the serpent had eaten itself from the tail on up. And she was glad. There was no remorse or guilt or pain in her spirit. This man's death did not erase the scars burned deep within her heart. It did not bring Miles back to life or ease the loneliness she'd felt since his life ebbed away. No, killing this man did not bring her a sense of satisfaction or even of completion; it merely drained her of the need for retribution and revenge. His bloody, lifeless corpse made her feel cold and numb inside, throwing water on the burning ache she'd carried since that night.

No, standing over the man who murdered her partner, killed another cop, and beat up her lover did not give her any great joy. She had done what any other cop in her position would have done; she preserved her life in the face of one who would have surely taken it from her.

What was it Megan had said? They do what they have to do to survive? Maybe they weren't so different afterall.

Bending over the corpse, Delta looked for the tattoo, but did not find it. She hadn't expected to find one. Like the whole cop killer story, it, too, was a phony.

As his eyes stared blankly at the ceiling of the warehouse, Delta knew they were the ones that glared at Miles down the barrel of a shotgun. She would never forget those eyes. And that one eye, the right one, wasn't it glass? Delta leaned over for a better look. Yes, it was glass.

"Damn you to the lowest depths of hell," Delta whispered, picking up the shotgun.

Looking out the windows and into the darkness, Delta felt the cold begin to thaw as the pilot light of her anger flared up. This man was of no use to her now. In saving herself, she blew away her pigeon. A different sort of smile played on Delta's face. Maybe he couldn't tell her what she needed to know, but one man could. The same man who had sentenced her to die in the warehouse: the man who emptied her shotgun, gave her a faulty radio, and left her to face a murderer alone.

Turning away from the corpse, Delta wiped the sweat from her palms. It was time she had a chat with Officer Taggart, and boy, would he be surprised to see her.

36

Making her way across the warehouse, Delta started for the window, but came to an abrupt halt. He would be waiting outside the window; waiting for the would-be killer to exit. Or maybe he was waiting to kill her himself. Surely, she was too dangerous to him now. He would have to kill her. He had no choice.

Turning around, Delta made her way to the other side of the building. All of the lower windows, with the exception of the entry window, had wrought iron bars, so they were out. The doors were also barred. Looking up, Delta saw some larger windows a few feet below the top of the scaffold. They were her only option. She could not afford to spend precious seconds looking for a way out.

Reaching the top of the scaffold, Delta laid on her stomach and peered out the window. She would have to break, jump, land, and draw in one smooth motion, ready to defend herself from a partner who had sent her to her death.

Taking the shotgun by one end, Delta lowered it to the window, swung it hard into the pane, busting glass and sending it everywhere. In the next instant, Delta was perched on the window sill, and without hesitation, she jumped.

As her feet crunched in the glass below, Delta rolled, dropped the shotgun, drew her side arm, and waited for Taggart to round the corner. As the sound of footsteps neared, Delta caught Taggart in her sights. She hated him more than the corpse in the warehouse. She hated him for selling out. In the darkest corner of her heart, Delta wished she had it in her to pull the trigger. If she hadn't needed him alive, she just might have.

When Taggart finally came into view, Delta aimed her gun at his chest.

"Stop, Taggart or I'll blow your fucking head off!"

"Stevens . . . am I glad—" Taggart stammered as he skidded to a halt. Delta saw his weapon in his right hand.

"Shut the fuck up. The game's over, you prick."

"Is it?" Taggart looked down at the weapon in his hand. His voice was challenging, but not strong.

"I wouldn't." Delta pressed her finger more firmly on the trigger. "I was a better shot than you in the Academy, and I still am. Draw on me, and you're a dead man."

Taggart hesitated a second, but did not drop the gun. "I got nothing to lose. They'll kill me anyway."

Delta raised her weapon to the same level as Taggart's head. "Then kiss your brains goodbye," Delta was not bluffing. As her finger started to press the trigger, Taggart flung his gun onto the ground.

"Okay, okay, there it is, there it is. Don't fuck around."

Delta did not lower her weapon. "You think I'm kidding around here? My real partner is dead. I'd just as soon you joined him."

"It's not what you—"

"Shut up! Don't fuck with me Taggart. I've already killed one man tonight. It won't take much to make it two."

Taggart slowly raised his hands into the air. "Easy, Stevens. "

"Easy, my ass. Lay your radio and the keys on the ground and walk away. I assume your radio works."

Taggart nodded as he withdrew the radio from the holder and placed it on the ground before tossing the keys next to it.

"Don't even think about running, Taggart. I will shoot you in the back if I have to."

"I ain't runnin'."

Delta bent over, still keeping her weapon on him, and picked up the radio. "Good for you. Maybe you're not so stupid afterall. Now, slowly take out your cuffs and put them on behind your back. Turn so I can see you putting them on. And remember — dropping you dead where you stand would be like wiping dog shit off my shoes." Taggart's hands were shaking as he slipped the handcuffs on, but he managed to lock them behind his back.

"Don't do this, Stevens—"

"Shut up! Now get down on your stomach."

As Taggart did as he was told, Delta pinched the cuffs tightly around his wrists to make sure they would not come off.

"Come on, Stevens, can't we cut a deal here?"

"Cut a deal? Cut a deal?" Delta kicked him in the side so he would roll over. "You must be insane if you think I would cut a deal with a scumbag like you. Don't talk to me about deals. You can do that with your lawyer."

Bending over him, Delta took the taping device out of her utility belt and taped it on his chest.

"What's that for?"

"Call it my ace in the hole." Turning the device on, Delta brought him to his feet. "Okay Taggart, where's the dope?"

For a second, he said nothing. Then, Delta jabbed her revolver into his ribs.

"Don't mess with me, Taggart. I'm working on limited patience here."

"It's at the Red Carpet."

"No shit. Where?"

"Room 315. Sometimes, it goes to room 317."

"When was the last shipment?"

Taggart shook his head, and Delta jabbed the nose back into his ribs.

"Yesterday. I think it was yesterday. I'm not sure. They've slowed way down since you've been sniffing around. But you're making a mistake, Stevens. They'll come after you."

"Good. That's exactly what I want." Jerking him around, Delta pushed him toward the patrol car. "You either cooperate with me, or your buddies'll find your body next to the ape's in the warehouse. Capishe?"

Taggart nodded.

"Good. You do everything exactly how I tell you. If you get out of line, even for a second, I'll blow your head off." Delta picked up the mike.

"What have you told them so far?"

Taggart shook his head. "Nothing. Really."

"Good. You tell them you have an officer down and need assistance. That's it. Any more and you're history."

Delta held both the mike and the gun up to Taggart's face, and he did as she ordered. When the radio jumped to life with response, she simply hung up the mike. Moving Taggart away from the unit, Delta picked up the mike, waited for clearance, and said in a low, gruff voice, "Checkmate." It was her signal to Connie that she was alright and they would proceed according to plan.

The radio dispatcher and several sergeants demanded to know who had said that, and the radio waves filled with excited chatter.

"What are you going to do with me?"

Checking his bugging device, Delta pressed a handcuff key into his palm. "That depends."

"I'll do whatever you want man, just stop waving that gun in my face."

Delta lowered her magnum and looked down at him. "Who's in this with you?"

Taggart looked away. As he did, Delta grabbed him by the collar and shoved him up against the wall.

"Don't waste my time, Taggart."

"Alright, alright. Patterson and McKlinton."

"That's all?"

Taggart looked away.

"Who else?"

Trembling, Taggart said in a low, near-whisper. "Owens, Larson, Chambliss. Come on, Stevens, you can't fight everyone."

"Don't make me have to shoot you to shut you up. Now, unlock your cuffs. All I want you to do is stand underneath that streetlight. When your backup buddies get here, you tell them that I'm dead. If you so much as let on otherwise, I'll fill you so full of lead, they'll use you as a ship's anchor. Understand?"

Taggart nodded.

Delta set the ear plug in her ear. She could hear his rapid breathing against the mike on his chest. "You go along just as you would have if I had been killed. Remember — one wrong move and your wife becomes a widow. And that would be a shame. She's such a pretty woman." Watching an uncuffed Taggart stand under the streetlight, Delta moved behind the patrol car and reloaded the shotgun. As she slammed the last round in, Patterson and McKlinton rolled up and jumped out of their car.

"Did he get her?"

Taggart nodded. "Yeah."

"She dead?"

"Yes."

Patterson sighed. "Too bad. She was a good cop."

"Yeah, a good cop on a suicide mission to find Brookman's killer," McKlinton offered. "She got in the way when she should've minded her own business."

Delta could still hear Taggart's chest heave up and down.

Suddenly, "Hey, Taggart, where's your gun?"

Before Taggart could respond, Delta jumped out from behind the car. "Move, and I'll drop you where you stand!"

All three men raised their hands in the air. Patterson and McKlinton turned and stared in amazement.

"What in the hell—" Patterson glared over at Taggart.

"I had to man, she was gonna kill me."

"Taggart, cuff them both," Delta ordered, keeping the shotgun aimed at the three men.

"Stevens, you've got this all wrong!"

"Save your breath guys," Taggart offered. "She got it all on tape."

Delta raised the shotgun to eye level and approached the circle of light cast by the streetlight. "I've killed one man tonight, and I won't hesitate to do it again."

Patterson and McKlinton stared at Taggart in disbelief. Taggart simply nodded.

"Taggart, take their guns out with your left hand and toss them in the bushes."

Taggart did so and stood awaiting her next order.

"You two, lay on the ground while he cuffs you."

"Stevens—"

"Shut up, Patterson. This whole damned thing is being recorded!"

"I don't give a fuck. She's crazy. She'll kill us all."

Delta chuckled. "That's quite possible, Mac. You've murdered my partner and beaten up my lover. Killing any of you would be a small price to pay, don't you think?" Delta watched carefully as Taggart recuffed himself. A small part of her wanted to shoot them all where they lay, but that would only lower her to their level.

"Stevens, listen to reason—"

"Reason? From you bastards? No, Mac, you listen. You may not have pulled the trigger when Miles was killed, but you were part of the bullet. For that, you'll pay for the rest of your lives."

"You know that tape don't mean a thing. It won't hold up in court."

Delta sighed. "You're right. Not by itself, it wouldn't. But I've got enough on you for a pretty airtight case."

"You think so? You don't even know who you're fucking with. You think we're the only ones?"

Delta grinned. They were so stupid. "You think I'm after just the little fish? Let me tell you something about reality, Patterson. Captain Williams, like all petty criminals, will leave you out to dry. You'll hang by your balls before he lets himself be busted for this." Delta sensed their desperation, their realization that the game, for them, was over. "So, if you think he'll bust one fingernail trying to help you assholes, guess again."

The three men said nothing.

"Now get in the back of my unit." Watching them struggle to their feet and move toward her car, Delta felt a twinge of sadness.

Once in the back of the car, Delta heard the sound of ambulance sirens on the way. They would find a body, of course, but thank God, it wouldn't be hers.

"While you three are back there, you might want to discuss how you can put an end to this thing. The District Attorney will look more favorably upon you if you cooperate."

"What are you going to do with us?"

Delta started the car and drove down the back streets to avoid the ambulance and other backup units. "I have a lot of work to do yet tonight, and I don't need you getting in my way."

"You're not going to kill us are you? We've cooperated so far."

Delta stopped the car and turned to glare at them through the mesh screen. "Cooperated? By the time I'm through with you, you'll be confessing to crimes you did when you were a child."

Wheeling back around, Delta parked in the court across from Connie's house, as planned. "You boys be good. I'll be back in a flash." Turning to the radio, Delta ripped the mike out. "And don't think there's a way out, because there isn't."

"Don't do this, Stevens," Patterson said, half begging, half threatening. "The Captain's got a whole lot more ammunition than you do. He can take you out like that."

"Shut the fuck up," Taggart growled. "I told you guys, she's got me wired. Everything you say—"

"Can and will be used against you in a court of law," Delta finished for him. So, Captain Williams was the top dog. So far, two of the three men had uttered his name in the wire. Victory was only two moves away.

Delta ran between two houses and around the back of one before ending up on Connie's front porch. From where she parked, the officers could not see the front door and did not know which house she went to.

The front door opened immediately, with Gina and Megan waiting.

"You're alright," Megan sighed, throwing her arms around Delta and hugging her tightly.

"I told you, I don't break promises." Kissing Megan's lips, Delta winked at Gina, who was putting on a down jacket.

"You ready?"

Gina and Megan nodded.

"I'm going with her," Megan said, grabbing her jacket off the peg. "You really shouldn't. You need—"

"I'll tell you what I need, sweetheart. I need to finish this with you."

Delta grinned. There was no use and no time to argue. Instead, she planted a quick kiss on Megan's cheek.

Gina opened the back door, and suddenly, two large-chested, extremely beefy Doberman pinschers bounded through the living room.

"All you have to do is make sure the guys stay in the car for a few more hours."

"And if they try to escape?"

"Let the dogs have them. If they make contact with Williams before Connic and I finish, you might as well order our tombstones."

Megan moved away from the two dogs heeling next to Gina.

"Don't worry on that count. Tasha and Cagney would rip them to pieces before they got halfway out of the car."

Delta nodded. "Good."

Megan slowly slid her hand into Delta's. "You are going to be alright now, aren't you?"

Delta brought Megan's hand to her lips and kissed it. "I wish I could say yes, but I just don't know." Delta looked down at her hands. She expected them to have blood dripping from them. "I had to kill the guy who was after me."

Megan pulled Delta to her. "I'm sorry."

"I didn't have much choice."

"You okay?" Gina asked.

"As good as someone can be who just shot a man." Looking up at Megan, Delta sighed heavily. "It was him or me."

"Then I'm glad you killed him." Pressing Delta to her, Megan lightly stroked her hair.

Gina patted Delta's back. "Are you off to the hotel, then?"

Delta nodded, slowly pulling away from the embrace. "Megan, you contact Connie and tell her what's happening. Have her call you back from a pay phone, though. I don't know if any of the station's phones are clean." Then, turning to Gina, Delta kissed her on the cheek. "You sure you and those dogs can take care of yourselves?"

"Honey, I'd rather have these dogs than that Magnum, any day."

"I figured as much. Okay, this is it." Delta hugged Megan and kissed her tenderly before threading her arm through Gina's and heading out the door.

"You be careful, Delta Stevens, do you hear me?"

"Loud and clear."

As Megan handed the keys to her car to Delta, she gripped her hand firmly. "I don't want to lose you."

Hugging her one last time, Delta whispered, "You won't. I'll be back."

Delta, Gina, and the two horse-dogs made their way through the neighboring backyard before ending up in front of the patrol car.

"Hi boys. This is Cagney, and this is Tasha. They're here to protect you."

"Protect us? From what?"

"From yourselves, of course. Should you decide to act foolishly, these dogs will treat themselves to dinner."

"Stevens, you won't get away with this. Think about it. By now, every man on the force is looking for us. You can't just keep us locked up here."

"Sure I can. Now don't get out of line, and you'll all have both arms and legs when I return."

"You crazy bitch! They'll kill you and everyone you know!"

Delta closed the door and made sure that all four doors were locked. With three large men in the back seat, there would be no room to maneuver in an effort to kick the window out.

"You'll be alright?" Delta asked Gina as she tethered the snarling dogs.

"Couldn't be safer. Get going now. Come home to us quickly."

37

Within minutes, Delta was at the hotel. By now, dispatch and everyone else in the world was wondering why there was one dead guy, one empty patrol car, and four missing cops; everyone except Captain Williams. His questions would be of a completely different nature. He would be in a major panic once he learned that his henchman was dead and three of his rotten apples gone. What he would be doing now, would be covering his tracks. Fear and panic ruled him now. The noose was tightening around his fat neck, and there was nothing he could do about it.

The thought made Delta smile.

Standing in front of room 315, Delta swallowed the lump in her throat. She could hear voices coming from inside; low, deep voices. There were at least two, maybe three, men inside. Delta smiled down at the shotgun in her hand. These men would do half the work for her.

Backing down the hall and around the corner, she steadied the shotgun on her left shoulder and waited for the door to open. They had to come toward her to either take the stairs or the elevator. Once they turned the corner, they were hers.

It was barely ten seconds before she heard them moving toward her. As three men rounded the corner carrying two large duffel bags, Delta aimed the shotgun at them.

"Move one eyelash and I'll blow your balls off," she growled at the three uniformed officers staring at her.

"Lower the bags to the ground, and then I want you, Larson, to take both their weapons out of their holsters with your left hand. Make an abrupt move and you're a dead man." Delta held the shotgun up and put slight pressure on the trigger as Larson eased one, two firearms out of their holsters and dropped them on the floor.

"Don't be stupid, Stevens," Larson said as he kicked both weapons across the carpet. "Join us and live. Believe me, it's more money than you'll ever—"

"Shut up. You're a dick, Larson, and I'll spit on your grave for what you did to Hammond. Now, slowly draw your weapon out with your left hand. Slowly, or I'll blow your hand off your wrist."

As Larson reached across his body with his left hand, Delta saw him turn his wrist around as he grabbed the gun's handle. Before the gun was completely released from the holster, Delta lowered her sights at his shins, pressed hard on the trigger, and shot Larson's legs out from under him. The other two cops hit the floor and covered their heads.

"Jesus! She's wacko!" Owens yelled, still covering his face.

"Hadn't you heard that I already killed one man tonight, you dumbass? "

Larson screamed in pain and writhed on the ground. Several doors on the floor opened, and seeing cops, people quickly closed up again.

"Owens, you take the two bags of dope. Chambliss, you pick your friend up and carry him down the stairs."

The two men did not move.

"Do it!" Bending down, keeping her eyes on them, Delta picked up the three weapons.

Both men immediately turned to the ordered task, and in less than a minute, they were inside Megan's room.

"Put him on the bed," Delta ordered.

"He's got to get to a hospital, man. He'll bleed to death."

"He'll do no such thing, " Delta retorted, still holding the shotgun at the two men. "I've seen pin pricks bleed more. He'll live. Cuff him to the bedpost."

Owens did as he was told.

"Now, cuff yourselves around the incinerator." Delta watched carefully as the two men did this. When they were through, she ordered them to wrap their legs around each other. When they had done this, she tore off some tape she'd used to tape Taggart's wire on, and placed a strip of tape over all three of their mouths.

"There. Tell me, is Williams expecting to hear from you?"

Both men nodded. Larson only continued to writhe on the bed.

"Will he come here if he thinks the dope is missing?"

The two men looked at each other and shrugged.

Delta picked up the phone and walked over to Owens. "You tell him that you're through and that if he wants the dope, he'll have to pick it up himself. Do you understand?"

Owens nodded.

"And do you understand that I'll blow your brains all over the room if you say anything else?"

Owens nodded again.

"Your fate is in your own hands. Saving Williams's ass isn't worth it." Laying the shotgun down, Delta pulled her sidearm and rested the end on Owens's temple. Delta could feel her heart racing as the beads of sweat dripped slowly down her back.

After ripping the tape off his mouth, Delta put the phone to Owens's ear and listened as he did exactly what she told him.

"Good boy."

"Let me go, Stevens, please. I have a wife and two kids."

"You should have thought about them before." Delta replaced the tape on his mouth.

Turning to leave, Delta stopped before she opened the door. "Someone should be here in a few hours to release you, so don't go anywhere."

Delta untied the knot to the duffel bags and began pulling several pre-wrapped bags of dope from the duffel. All three packages still had evidence tags on them. No wonder Williams was moving this dope so fast. It had not yet been repackaged. It was more than she had hoped for. Now, she had six prisoners, three bags of dope, conversations on tape, and one more fish to net before this was all over.

Picking up the phone, Delta called Connie.

"I'm at the white queen's," Delta said in their prear-ranged chess code.

"Thank God, I've been going out of my mind here. You okay?"

"Yep. How's your end?"

Connie punched a message into Eddie that would go straight into Bear's computer. "It's a madhouse around here. Something about a dead man in a warehouse and four missing cops. You sure know how to create a stir. Go."

"White knight to black bishop." Delta heard Connie punch in more information.

"Black king to white queen, in less than five." Connie responded. This meant that the Captain, the black king, was just now leaving the office and probably heading for the hotel.

"White bishop also to white queen in five. White knight must be clear."

Delta nodded. The white bishop was Bear. He, too, would be heading for the vicinity of the hotel.

"Will do. And white rook?"

"White rook to recall black pawns. After that, white knight is solo."

Delta nodded again. Connie, the white rook, her favorite piece, was going to dispatch and have them reroute any cops who were anywhere around the hotel. She did not want any interference to keep the final move from happening. That was Connie's job. This would leave Delta, Williams, and Bear for the showdown.

"Thanks. See you in a bit."

"You'd better."

Grabbing one of the duffel bags, Delta headed for the back entrance. This was where the timing element was critical. Delta figured she had about one minute to operate before he returned to his car, empty-handed and angry. She could not afford a mistake here.

As Williams pulled up, Delta smiled. Even better than she had hoped. He had driven his own vehicle. This couldn't be sweeter.

The second he entered the hotel, Delta hoisted the duffel over her shoulder, zipped behind cars, until she came to his. Pulling out her jimmy, she had the trunk unlocked in seconds. Popping open the trunk, Delta heaved the dope in and tossed in three stray, well-tagged packages. One of the packages landed on a piece of yellow paper that Delta picked up. It was Williams's asthma prescription. Staring at the piece of paper, Delta crammed it into her pocket and continued her work.

After dropping in all the dope, Delta found the wires to the taillight and pulled them out. Bear would then pull Williams over because of a malfunctioning taillight. Instead of issuing a fix it ticket, Bear would mention to Williams that it was probably just a loose wire and have Williams open the trunk. Not knowing that there was almost one hundred pounds of already-seized dope in the back of his car, Williams would do as Bear asked. The thought of the look on his face when he discovered the dope in his car made Delta smile. She would love to be there.

Delta had just enough time to close the trunk and scoot behind two parked cars before Williams pushed through the door. He appeared both angry and confused. His dope was gone, his officers were missing, and he hadn't a clue as to what to do to save his ass.

The whole idea brought tears of anger to Delta's eyes.

It would only be a minute before Bear pulled him over. After that, Bear would take him to the county jail, where it was a matter of hours before the others raced to their lawyers to begin pleabargaining. Rats may jump a sinking ship, but they'd step all over each other to be the first ones off.

Delta counted on this.

38

When Delta returned to Connie's place, Gina, Megan, and the dogs sat huddled on the sidewalk, still watching over the three men in back. As soon as Delta was out of the car, Megan ran to her.

"Did we do it? Is it over?"

Delta nodded. "Just about."

Gina and the dogs joined them. "Did we get him?"

"I'd say, right about now, he's being hauled off to the county jail with about a hundred pounds of evidence dope. He's got an awful lot of explaining to do."

Gina, too, hugged Delta.

"These guys haven't given you any problems?"

Gina laughed. "They haven't moved."

"Did they talk?"

Both Megan and Gina nodded. "A lot."

"Good."

"What are you going to do with them now?"

"Watch." Delta opened up the back door and motioned for Patterson to get out.

"No way, Stevens. I ain't lettin' those hounds take a bite outta me."

"Get out, you moron. I'm not going to sic the dogs on you. It's over. Williams has confessed the entire thing."

"You're lying."

"Am I?"

The three men slowly got out of the car, keeping a wary eye on the two growling dogs.

"I'm going to unlock Taggart's cuffs and let him unlock yours. I have no more need of you." Delta stepped up to Taggart and ripped his mike off his chest. Then she leaned over into the front and pulled out the recorder. "Before you go running to your lawyers, I think you should go to room 102 at the Red Carpet and free your buddies."

The cops exchanged glances, but said nothing, as Delta pressed a handcuff key into Taggart's hand.

"Oh, and call an ambulance for Larson. I had to shoot him."

Taggart swore under his breath as he unlocked the other two.

"You're crazy."

Delta shrugged. "Maybe I am. But I'm alive and I'm free, which is more than you'll be in the next twenty-four hours."

"You don't expect us to believe you actually have Williams in custody?"

"I really couldn't give a shit what you believe. The game is over and you've lost. If I were you, I'd be trying to figure a way of shortening my sentence."

Taggart took a step toward Delta. Cagney and Tasha bared long white fangs and jerked at the leather leash.

"Now don't try anything fellas, these dogs don't seem to like you too well." Delta smiled as the two dogs growled menacingly. The leather strap pulled taut, Gina stepped closer to the men, who instantly backed off.

"Okay, okay, ease the dogs off."

Tossing Taggart the keys to the unit, Delta stepped next to Gina and the dogs.

"You can't know how much we'd love to let these dogs loose on you, but I've got other plans. I'll see you all burn in court. Now get the hell out of here."

The three men jumped into the patrol car as Cagney and Tasha pulled harder on the heavy leather leash.

"There's one thing that's been bugging the shit out of me all night long, Stevens," Taggart said, rolling down the window of the car.

"What's that?"

"I heard three shots in the warehouse. There was one, and then a long pause, and then two right after each other. Did you shoot him three times?"

Suddenly, Delta looked down at her chest. There were no bloodstains at all. Only a small, round hole in her left chest pocket. "Actually, Taggart, he shot me once. Now go."

As the car sped off, Delta turned to find Gina and Megan staring in disbelief.

"You've been shot?" Megan asked slowly, moving closer to Delta.

Still looking at the hole, Delta's eyes welled up with tears. Putting her index finger into the hole, Delta knew, even before she felt it, the reason there was no blood and no wound. With her finger in the hole, Delta closed her eyes.

"Honey, are you okay?" Gina asked, stepping up to Delta and laying her hand on Delta's shoulder. "You were shot, weren't you?"

Delta nodded. Looking up from the hole and seeing a blur, Delta nodded again. "Yes, Gina, I was. It was a perfect shot by a .357 Magnum practically at point blank range. It should have gone right through my heart."

Megan quickly sat on the ground. "Oh my God."

Squatting next to Megan, Delta ran her hand through Megan's hair. "But it didn't. Didn't even scratch me." Helping Megan to her feet, Delta pulled both women to her and hugged them tightly.

Reaching into her left chest pocket, Delta withdrew Miles's badge and held it out for them to see.

"I've been carrying it around with me since he died." Delta turned it over and examined it. Right in the middle of the badge was a huge dent made by the bullet meant for her heart.

"This is what the bullet hit."

For a long, quiet moment, the three women stood, sharing a secret silence. For a deep, metaphysical second, all three women felt a presence surrounding them, loving them, showing them that the spirit never really dies; that love goes on even when the shell from which it came is gone. In that quiet moment under the streetlight and clouded skies, Delta understood the true power of love and friendship.

Still staring down at dented badge number 342, Delta cried.

39

The next morning, Delta walked into the District Attorney's office, evidence in hand. District Attorney Alexandria Pendleton stood up from behind her huge desk as Delta was escorted in by the receptionist.

"I understand you have some information regarding last night's arrest of your Captain."

D.A. Pendleton had long auburn hair that swirled past her shoulders, delicately stroking the teal silk blouse she was wearing. Delta extended her hand out and shook her strong grip. Her gray-green eyes locked onto Delta, as if examining her. Her perfume, like her presence, was strong.

"Yes, I do." Delta laid a manilla folder on the desk and sat down in the brown leather chair opposite the District Attorney's.

"Is there anything in there I can use?"

"Are you asking if it was illegally obtained?"

The D.A. smiled. "Something like that. I've spent all morning on the phone. Apparently there are a lot of people at the station who believe he was set up. What do you think?"

Delta did not blink. "I think the evidence speaks for itself."

"Not necessarily. I want you to speak for it. Because if I find out that you or your colleagues so much as thought about setting him up, I'll have your badge. Do you read me?"

Delta nodded, not taking her eyes off the penetrating gaze of the D.A.

"We can't have vigilantes running around our city."

"I understand that."

District Attorney Pendleton leaned over her desk. "Do you? I would assume, if you do, that you'll be able to convince me why this information wasn't brought to my immediate attention, instead of me having to hear about it on this morning's news."

Leaning back, Delta scratched her nose.

"There was nothing you could have done. Their plan was practically foolproof. They even had a scapegoat set up should anyone become suspicious. That scapegoat, Ms. Pendleton, was my dead partner."

The D.A. leaned back in her chair and studied Delta a moment before replying. "And you can prove these allegations about your partner being set up? Because if you can't, there's going to be an investigation into your activities so deep, you'll never see the sky again."

Delta smiled. She liked the hard-line attitude District Attorney Pendleton was taking with her. It meant she was thorough, exact, and wouldn't let vital information or evidence slip through her fingers. That was good.

"I'm sure, once you hear the tape and see the story unfold, you'll understand why it had to be this way."

"Then by all means, Officer Stevens, enlighten me." Draping her arm across the chair, The District Attorney waited.

For the next thirty minutes, Delta told her story while the D.A. took notes. Except for the placing of the dope in Williams's car and Bear's involvement, Delta's narrative was succinct and to the bone, if not completely forthright.

When Delta finished, the D.A. leaned across the desk over her folded hands. Her eyes narrowed, and her pupils were small and hard. "Do you have this tape?"

Delta nodded. "Everything is in that folder."

Alexandria Pendleton had been the District Attorney for three years, and never in her time in office, had she ever heard a tape that so shook her as the one Delta played for her now.

"My god," the D.A. murmured, leaning back in her large, leather chair as Taggart and Patterson spoke in near hysterics about how to get themselves out of the murder conviction. She gasped when McKlinton said they should have killed Delta that rainy night they took Miles out. And she sighed sadly when she heard Patterson wonder out loud what he would tell his children. It was all there. An hour or so of conversation by condemned men who had painted themselves into a corner with the blood of two fine men.

"Officer Stevens, I . . . don't quite know what to say."

Delta folded her hands in her lap and sighed. "Horrifying, isn't it?"

Alexandria Pendleton shook her head slowly. "Unbelievable. Cops killing cops."

Delta leaned on the desk. She wanted D.A. Pendleton to understand the magnitude of this case. "No, Ms. Pendleton — dirty cops killing good, clean cops. There's a big difference."

The D.A. was still shaking her head. "It makes me sick to think about it. And you're telling me that Miles Brookman and James Hammond were killed by the man found in the warehouse; the man who was also sent to allegedly murder you?"

Delta nodded. "There were other people in the van the night Miles was killed. Could have been cops. Could have just been his buddies getting off on a cold-blooded murder."

Opening the folder, Pendleton took out the matchbook, the list, the printout of the evidence sign-outs and laid them on her desk. For a silent minute, she stared down at the evidence before her. "You've been awfully busy, haven't you?"

"He was my partner." Delta didn't know what else to say.

The District Attorney nodded. "I understand. I'm just not sure I, myself, would have had the courage to do what you've done."

"You'd be surprised what you can do when you see someone you love shot down right in front of you."

The D.A. visibly shuddered at the thought. "Well, you've done your job well. I believe it's my turn." D.A. Pendleton stood up and offered her hand to Delta.

"There's one last bit that you might want to look into."

D.A. Pendleton's eyebrows raised. "You never give up, do you?"

Delta shook her head. "No, I don't."

Pulling the yellow slip of paper she found in Williams's trunk, Delta handed it to the D.A.

"What's this?"

"It's a prescription Williams had for asthma."

"What's the catch?"

"Before Miles was killed, we were talking about the fact that we didn't have a clue as to how the dope was being funneled back into the streets. We shook down every street corner pusher and dealer for blocks, and still came up empty. We squeezed every possible source we had, and still, no one knew where it was coming from."

D.A. Pendleton looked at the yellow slip. "What better place to deal drugs from, than a pharmacy?"

Delta nodded. "Once you haul this man in, you've got your key witness."

"Makes sense. A dirty cop would feel easier about dealing with white collar criminals than with street people. You've done exceptional work, Officer Stevens."

"The name is Delta."

"Well, Delta, you do realize the role you'll have to play in the trial? You may not come out of this with any colleagues. Even good cops don't like snitches."

Delta nodded. "I know. This wasn't a popularity contest Ms. Pendleton. I just finished the job my partner started, that's all." Rising, Delta took D.A. Pendleton's hand firmly in hers. "It's your baby now."

Pendleton smiled. "I'll give it everything I've got. I do have just one more question for you."

Tired, sore, and not sure she was up to any more questions, Delta nodded. "What's that?"

"Why?"

Delta cocked her head. "Why?"

"Yes. Why? What happens to good cops that makes them turn sour?"

Still standing, Delta backed away from the desk and stared out the window. A gentle mist stroked the pane. "I read a poem once by a black poet. Can't remember his name right now. It was subtitled *What Happens to a Dream*

Deferred? I think cops have incredible dreams when they come out of the Academy. We have energy, enthusiasm, and a love for what's good and right."

"And then?"

"God," the word seemed to fall out of Delta's mouth. "And then you face the dregs of society day in and day out. Sometimes, these people are making more money in one day than we'll see in a month. You bust your ass, take a few stitches, maybe watch a man lose his life, only to see the same scum back on the street because some high-priced lawyer maneuvered around a leaky system. All your work, all your energy ends up being for nothing. It gets to you after a while, I guess. Some cops escape with alcohol, some lift weights, and . . ."

"And some give in."

Delta nodded, still gazing outside. For a moment, she had forgotten Alexandria Pendleton was in the room.

"How do you cope with it, Delta?"

"Cope? You don't really cope. You cope when a child dies in your arms, or when you hold a woman who has just been raped. That's when you cope, that's when you better believe in something more powerful than yourself." Delta watched three young girls walk across the crosswalk holding hands. "How do you stay clean? That comes from within." As Delta watched the girls get on a bus, she felt Alexandria's hand touch her shoulder.

"Well, Delta Stevens, whatever you believe in, wherever your inner strength comes from, I applaud it. You are one hell of a woman."

For a moment, the two women stood by the window, looking out at whatever dreams and emotions drifted past. Delta watched as the mist started falling in heavier drops and sighed as they rolled quickly down the pane.

"I'll do everything I can do get you a conviction on this, Delta."

"Thank you."

Turning to leave, Delta stopped, hand poised on the shiny brass knob. "You know, the last line of the poem asks whether or not a dream deferred just explodes. What do you think?"

Alexandria Pendleton stepped out from behind her desk and stood a foot away from Delta.

"I think that people like you keep that from happening."

Smiling her acceptance of the compliment, Delta walked out of the office.

Before she could reach her car, three large men in blue were lumbering toward her. "Shit," Delta muttered to herself, seeing them approach. It was starting already.

"Hey, Stevens!" one of the officers called.

Delta swallowed hard. "What, Quince?"

The larger man known as Quince walked over to her and stuck his hand out. "The guys in the department heard what you did last night. Took a lot of guts to take them on by yourself."

Delta's jaw dropped open.

"Taking down dirty cops is bad business, but it's gotta be done. We just wanted to congratulate ya."

Delta slowly reached out to the huge hand and shook it.

"I don't know all the particulars, but we've heard that you busted some kinda drug operation. From the inside."

Delta nodded, still speechless.

"Well, we just wanted you to know that the three of us are behind you. You're okay in our book."

"Yeah, and if any of the other guys give you any shit, you come to us, okay? It's shit like this that gives us all a bad name. We gotta stand by each other."

Inhaling slowly, Delta nodded again. "You don't know how much this means to me."

Quince winked at her. "You're a damn good cop, Stevens. And I'd have you for a partner any day. I'm sorry that Miles and James were offed by those assholes. Never liked that damned Williams anyway. Always had that shifty look in his eye."

Delta nodded and grinned. She sensed the helplessness these men were feeling — their impotence to keep a friend from harm. She knew that feeling — she had spent many a night crying it out of her soul.

"I appreciate this a lot, you guys. I wasn't sure if I had any friends left."

Quince laid his hand on Delta's shoulder. "More than you know. It took more courage than I've got to do what you did. A man's gotta admire someone with that kind of chutzpah."

"Yeah. I got a wife and kids."

Delta smiled, feeling the heat of humility rise to her face. "Thanks."

"No, Stevens. Thank you. And remember that we're here. Us and lots of the other guys as well."

Watching the three men stride away, Delta heaved a sigh. Finally, she and Connie were no longer lone figures fighting the system.

Checkmate.

Game over.

40

On the fourth day after Williams's arrest, Delta rose from her own bed and found Megan cooking breakfast in the kitchen. On Pendleton's advice, Delta had taken a leave of absence in order to stay out of the limelight as long as possible. Thus far, in the four days since Williams's arrest, five cops had been arrested, and two resigned from the force. The dominoes were quickly falling.

"Mmm, don't you look good enough to eat," Delta said, threading her arms around Megan's waist. "What's cooking?"

Turning while still in Delta's arms, Megan kissed her long and hard.

"Nothing, yet. Want some eggs?" Megan winked sensually.

Pulling Megan away from the kitchen and into the living room, Delta shook her head.

"I know I've done nothing but sleep the last three days, but I'm awake now, and I have a few things to say to you."

Megan sat on the couch next to Delta and held her hand.

"You have been so wonderful through all this, that I don't know how to thank you."

Megan's blue eyes sizzled. "I thought Hawaii was on the agenda."

Smiling, Delta nodded. "So it is. But before you and I go any further, I think there are some things I must say."

The fire in Megan's eyes cooled, and she nervously grabbed Delta's hand in both of hers. "I think I know what this is about."

Delta smiled gently and retrieved one of her hands so she could stroke Megan's soft cheeks. "Yes, but I don't think you have any idea the direction it's headed."

Megan's eyes widened. "Maybe I don't want to know. I've been dreading this talk. I kept hoping that when this was all over, you and I could just move ahead. I . . . I guess I've just been fooling myself, haven't I?"

Delta slowly shook her head. "No. I don't think so."

A tiny flicker of light shone in Megan's eyes. "No?"

"No. Megan, since you've come into my life, I feel so alive again. It's been a long time since someone has touched me as you have, and I'm not about to toss those feelings to the wind. I'm not the same woman who started digging where Miles left off. So much of that change I owe to you."

Megan silenced Delta with a finger to her lips. "You don't need to thank me, sweetheart."

"Yes I do. Before you came into my life, I only saw the world in terms of black and white. I suppose being a cop made me predisposed to that way of thinking, but since being with you, I've realized that it doesn't need to be that way."

Megan ran her hands through Delta's hair and brushed her fingers across her cheek. "Oh, Delta, you don't know how happy it makes me to hear that. I was so afraid—"

"So was I. I was so afraid that I was going to throw us away because we come from opposite ends of the universe. And maybe I would have. Maybe being a cop was all I knew. Maybe I had become black and white. But I learned a great deal about myself when I was trying to stay alive in that warehouse. When I killed that man, I realized that I did what I had to do to survive. For the first time, I understood what you meant."

"We're not so different, you and me."

Delta smiled. "No, we're not. Not anymore."

Pulling Megan to her, Delta kissed her, gently at first, but then, harder, thrusting her tongue into Megan's mouth.

Pushing Delta away, Megan fanned herself. "Why, Officer Stevens, I do believe you care for me."

Bringing Megan back to her, Delta kissed her warmly. "Yes, Megan Osbourne, I most certainly do."

"Enough to do that one thing?"

Delta's eyes grew wide. Licking her lips, she nodded vigorously. "Oh God, yes."

"Good!" Jumping to her feet, Megan left the room and quickly returned carrying a square board with chess pieces on top. Setting it on the table, Megan sat across from Delta, who looked at the chessboard bemused.

"Is this that 'one thing' you were talking about?"

Megan's eyes sparkled. "Well, of course. What *one thing* did you think I meant?" Winking, Megan leaned across the table, knocking some pieces to the floor and slipped her hand into Delta's pajama top. "Why don't you make the first move?" Megan murmured huskily.

For Delta, it was the sweetest chess match she ever played.

41

When the guilty verdicts were handed down and the lengthy sentences pounded out with the gavel, Delta found herself driving alone to the cemetery. The trial, as anticipated, had not been long. The evidence and various plea bargaining was sufficient enough to lock most of them behind bars for a long, long time. The pharmacist's testimony buried Williams, as he had kept a log of dates, times and transactions Williams and others had made. Jennifer came to the trials every day, as did Connie and Megan. It was an emotionally difficult trial because friends were called in to testify against friends and partners against partners. But in the end, the individuals standing on the two sides of the issue were clearly divided.

When it was finally over, there was no celebration or cork-popping. While Delta was glad to see justice done, the price everyone paid, they paid in spirit. It was that very spirit that Delta needed to mend now.

Standing by Miles's grave, Delta sighed heavily. The rains made the surrounding grass smell fresh and clean, and birds chirped as a slight breeze rustled the leafless branches. Looking about her, Delta felt alive, and she knew that Miles wanted her to feel alive.

"It's me again," she said, taking her hand from her pocket. "We did it. It took a lot of work, but we did it. I told you I wouldn't let you down." Delta looked around her at the other visitors. "My life is very different now, without you. I've fallen in love with Megan. Somehow, I think you expected that to happen. Maybe, in some weird way, you had a hand in it." Inhaling, Delta released a loud sigh. "I miss you, big guy, but it's time for me to move on. I need to know that I've let go of you. My therapist said it would be good for me. I finally had to agree. So . . . here I am, one last time, to say goodbye."

Laying three objects on the headstone, Delta wiped her eyes. A tiny rain tumbled carelessly to the ground. Standing two of the objects up, Delta removed her hand from the white king and the white knight; two marble pieces from the chess set Miles bought for her.

"Do they play much chess where you are?" Delta asked, centering the third object in the middle. "If they do, always remember that the best moves are often the most preposterous, illogical, and outlandish ones imaginable."

Staring down at the middle object, Delta closed her eyes. "Your badge saved my life, my friend, and for that gift, I can promise you to live it to the fullest." Delta paused for a moment. "I don't think I'll ever have another partner who means as much to me as you did. And I'll take all the things we learned together and use them to make my little corner of the world safer for your kids. And when your children ask what kind of man you were, I'll tell them you were the bravest, most sensitive, and most wonderful man I've ever met. I'll tell them that you were the best friend a woman could have. I love you, Miles. I'll always love you."

As Delta walked away, the tiny drops of rain gently glided down and rolled off dented badge number 342.

ABOUT THE AUTHOR

Linda Kay Silva was born and raised in Danville, California. She still resides in Danville with two cats, the Mother and the Boyfriend. She has been teaching Middle School English and History for the past seven years. Prior to that, she was a cop in Alameda County.

During her spare time, Linda officiates high school sports, works out, travels, and writes constantly. She is currently working on three sequels to TAKEN BY STORM, and she has completed another manuscript about a lesbian couple in Nazi Poland.

PARADIGM

Publishing
Company

P.O. Box 3877
San Diego, CA 92163
Brenda Hines/Deanna Leach

Paradigm Publishing Company was recently founded to publish works created within communities of diversity.

A paradigm is one's perception of reality which is generally formed out of one's experiences and cultural traditions. We firmly believe that the paradigms of mainstream society need to be continually critiqued and challenged, and new paradigms created. This work has generally been best accomplished by communities of diversity which have been placed on the fringes of mainstream society because of their diversity. However, their voices have been silenced by inaccessability to traditional publishing avenues.

Therefore, Paradigm Publishing has joined the network of small presses dedicated to providing diverse communities with access to being published and being heard. We encourage their diversity and encourage these communities to tell their own stories, thereby empowering themselves and society by the creation of new paradigms which are inclusive of diversity.

We welcome manuscripts from any diverse community: people of color, lesbians, gays, differently abled, and feminists.

* * * * * * * *

Other Books Published by Paradigm Publishing:

Expenses by Penny S. Lorio
ISBN 0-9628595-0-8 $8.95